Barua, Kaushik,
No direction Rome /
2017

37565028406998

1/13 ℰω

S0-BRY-446

OFFICIAL
DISCARD

LIBRARY

peta

NO
DI←
REC→
TION
ROME

KAUSHIK BARUA

NO DI← REC→ TION ROME

THE PERMANENT PRESS
Sag Harbor, NY 11963

Copyright © 2017 by Kaushik Barua

All rights reserved. No part of this publication, or parts thereof, may be reproduced in any form, except for the inclusion of brief quotes in a review, without the written permission of the publisher.

For information, address:
    The Permanent Press
    4170 Noyac Road
    Sag Harbor, NY 11963
    www.thepermanentpress.com

Library of Congress Cataloging-in-Publication Data

    Barua, Kaushik, author.
        No direction Rome / Kaushik Barua.
        Sag Harbor, NY: The Permanent Press, [2017]
        ISBN: 978-1-57962-512-2
            1. Black humor (Literature) 2. Humorous fiction.

    PR9499.4.B372 N6 2017
    823'.92—dc23   2017017405

Printed in the United States of America

To Deuta

September 2012

TALKING TO DEER

On Friday afternoon, Pooja tried to kill herself. But the canal wasn't deep enough. She stood up, surprised, and tried to walk back to the edge. Then she slipped and hit her head against the wall.

Saturday was a blur. There were policemen on cycles with neon yellow jackets, tubes crisscrossing the air in front of her face in hospital, all starting in some pouch and ending inside her, her mother's screaming face inches from mine with freshly minted rage she had brought all the way from India, my retreat—no, my charge—to the airport where I told the check-in attendant with her breasts straining against her name tag—Marina—that I was on holiday but my fiancée liked Amsterdam so much she decided to stay on for a few days, the taxi ride back from the airport in Rome when I stared at the bald patch on the driver's head with an open sore in the middle that looked like herpes or one of those unnamable STDs.

On Sunday, I rested. Does that sound too grand? As if I'm talking about the God you pretend not to believe in, the one with the long white beard and a face like Charlton Heston. He may even look like Morgan Freeman, but definitely not like Winona Ryder. On the seventh day, He rested. Anyway, on Sunday, I slept. On Monday, I took the day off. And by noon, I was already stoned.

I had to meet a few friends in the evening. Not friends really, members of this Rome Expat Socialising Club. I walked down the gently sloping Via Claudia till I came upon the Colosseo standing massive and jagged in front of me. I had to walk all the way round the thing to reach the centre of the city. I didn't know what the Colosseo was still doing there. It had been around for 2,000 years, I remembered reading, its massive open mouth gaping at the skies like a toilet bowl for the gods. The gods taking a dump on us all for 2,000 years. Once they had gladiators in fifty-kilo armour fighting for their lives here. Now they have freckled American college kids ooh-ing and aah-ing before getting pissed in the bars near my place. I hated them all. Also, none of them ever made it to my bed; though I walked past them often and even asked for directions to random streets. I don't think any of them were cool enough for me. Not that I ever had a gladiator in my bed, so I wouldn't really know about them either.

But of course I wasn't thinking about American college kids. I was thinking about Pooja. A week before she took the plunge, we were signing forms to get married. When she was conscious in hospital, I asked her why. I wasn't crying, but I was serious. And she said it wasn't about me.

She tried to kill herself and it wasn't about me? That really took my trip.

I stopped near the supermarket. There was no one to ask for directions. No Italian aunty on stubby legs with the corner of her milk packet tearing against the natural-plastic bag; no girl jabbing on her phone at the bus stop; no men with cultivated stubbles and earpieces jammed in their ears, their hands all over the place fervently plucking words out of the air; not even middle-aged tourists with teenage kids making family history in front of the epic toilet bowl. The restaurants were full, but the waiters had all seen me before. So I continued on my own to the red light and turned left.

Then I saw him, the first candidate of the day. An old man, gaunt in a sexy kind of way, with grey hair that curled over his ears, wearing one of those elbow-patch jackets—he was stuffing tobacco into his pipe. I asked him if he knew the way to Via del Corso. He handed me his pipe, and raised both hands in intricate gestures as he spoke. I wondered about his life. Sometimes, I thought, he met his friends from the village in Tuscany and they spoke about what was going wrong with the country. He told them how everything worked better in the United States and even in China where his cousin stayed. After drinks in the bar where the bartender knew all the wines and all the customers by origin and vintage, he walked back home with his wife and they tried to make love but often failed. When she was away at her mamma's place he would pull down his stack of magazines and try to jerk off but so many of the pages were stuck together it was difficult. When he was done or not done and he could feel his always-sore knees again, he would still be thankful he married his wife and not one of the paper girls.

His daughter-in-law looked like one of those paper girls. Yes, he sometimes leched at her. But never at his daughter, that would be a sin. I might lech at my daughter-in-law. I don't think Pooja ever would, I mean lust for a son-in-law. She was too serious that way. Taking too much load. It's a wonder she didn't sink.

The old man finished giving me directions and I handed him back his pipe. I smiled at him, as if to let him know that everything was good. Life was good; he had nothing to fear. I have a lot of love for strangers sometimes. I'm very Buddhist in that way. I'm not sure he got my message. It was a bit too subliminal. Not too many people got the Buddha's message either. The Buddha spent many years talking to deer in the forests.

When I reached Fori Imperiali, I found a lady. She had huge square shades and looked like Blade Runner. Or was that Blade? I asked her for directions—Via del Corso? She shook her shoulders and looked skyward. I looked up too; she was gone before I looked back. Probably hunting teenage vampires. There was a grey gurgling sky overhead. Once I rented a car whose roof slid down; Pooja and I drove to the Amalfi Coast. She threw her head back and laughed. She was a 1970s Bollywood girl. Her teeth were porcelain. I heard teeth grow forever. I would say something stupid and she'd laugh. Then I'd try my wry smile, slightly crooked. She loved that. The water didn't kill her, the wall didn't kill her, but life will get her in the end. Don't burn me, she said, don't let them burn me when I die. Someday the world will be covered in porcelain. But I won't be there.

The Rome Expat Socialising Club was waiting. Blade didn't know the way. But like always, I did. I walked past Trajan's market. It had a crescent of crumbling rooms, four stories of them. In the semidarkness, the walls turned deep maroon like they might have looked when the ancient Romans were trading cattle or armour or whatever they needed. Or gladiator prostitutes.

Someone touched my elbow, I mean tapped it, not stroked it or anything. I saw a Bangladeshi with a tower of fluorescent Colosseos growing out of his left hand and my elbow growing out of his right.

Where are you going? He said it in English, Via del Corso?

I didn't reply. I didn't like talking to these Bangladeshi vendors. Or the Indian ones. In case they got the wrong ideas. I don't know what ideas, but the wrong ones. Like I'm their brother or something.

Dove vai? Dove vai?

I didn't speak much Italian, but I wouldn't have replied anyway.

Straight, go straight, *sempre dritto*. He continued. I nodded him away; but he stayed a few steps behind me. How did he speak English so well?

Do you like cricket? Tendulkar?

No, no cricket.

I hated it when people presumed I was Indian, or that I liked cricket, and assumed I liked Sachin Tendulkar, the twenty-year resident god of Indian cricket.

I hurried on, but I could still hear the Bangladeshi behind me. The Twenty20 Cricket World Cup is coming, he yelled. Once I looked back and his eyes were following some girl's ass. Perv. Then he started humming an old Bollywood song: *Jeena yahan, marna yahan, iske siva jaana kahan* . . . To live here, and to die here, where else is there to go? The world is filled with weirdos.

I tried walking faster. I didn't look back till I reached the bar. By then, the humming had been drowned out by the city. I thought I heard someone shout out Mr. India when I walked in, but I wasn't sure.

I found the group I was looking for; silicon smiles flared across the table. It was a large group: fourteen, maybe fifteen. Massimo was there. He was from the office. But he was a friend. He spent half the day researching important global issues: the most violent animals in the world, the coolest animals who didn't give a fuck, or film stars who looked the same in every poster, like Tom Cruise's side profile. Sometimes he did a little work. Smarter than the system, that's my only fault, he would say. He never got caught he was so good at switching screens. He could hear footsteps twenty feet away and switch screens. He was the Alt-Tab man; that was his superpower.

And there was Liesbeth, the Dutch girl. She worked in Africa a lot, doing some development project. Her Facebook was filled with photos of babies with swollen bellies. Half the time they were in her arms. I liked the photos. I mean, I "like"d them. And then I would "like" the whole album. I made sure I didn't like every photo, only about half. There was a baby with eyes like Charlie Chaplin and a Sumo belly. It looked like he was reaching for her breasts. I liked that one.

The Indian girl came up to me. Maya, she was Indian-American, second generation or whatever you call them, the ones who are filled with angst and a longing for a home-land they don't even know. But that's a different story. And I don't really care about that story.

What happened to your friend? Your family friend? She meant Pooja. She knew we were having an arranged mar-riage. Maya probably laughed about it and told everyone else.

She's gone back home, I said. She wanted to spend some time with her family.

I know how that feels, Maya said.

I'm sure you do.

She didn't spend much time on me. I saw her scurry back to the group. She was reading the wine menu with two other girls. And they were whispering to each other. One laughed. I think Maya looked back towards me. I reached for the vodka tonic and nudged Massimo to a corner.

What happened? he asked me, I got your text. Everything okay?

She's gone. Gone back home; her mom came to Amsterdam to pick her up.

Mom picked her up? So the marriage is off?

I don't know. Maybe she doesn't want to hurry. I didn't want to get married anyway.

Did you guys do it? Wasn't that why you went to Amsterdam together? So did you do it?

Almost.

Which means you held hands?

No, which means I pulled it out, last minute.

I thought that sort of thing doesn't happen with your arranged marriage scene.

The pulling out?

No, the sex before marriage, because you don't really know each other.

I knew her. I got to know her.

So the sex happening isn't so rare?

Stranger things have happened. And I think she started liking me.

And you?

I guess. She was nice, but slightly messed up.

Why don't you call her? Is she coming back to her job in London? Maybe you guys can still meet. Even try dating? Like normal people?

Maybe I will. I don't want to lose any of my options.

How many options do you have?

Enough.

You mean right hand or left hand?

Shut up, Massimo.

He laughed. The two spots on his temple lit up. When Massimo was a teenager, he crashed his bike. He had broken his skull into twenty pieces; they screwed it back, held together with a steel frame. He spent more than a month in hospital. His mamma prayed for forty days, kneeling in the pews of her church, hands together, nails scraping each other clean. When he went back to school, he had all the girls pitying him, rubbing his back. But that's not where he wanted their hands.

His mamma found his marijuana tree when he was in hospital. She let it grow. If that will bring him back, let it stay, she thought. And he came back, with a spaceship on his head for a year.

Mamma died when he moved to Rome. Not because he moved to Rome, though one never knows with Italian mammas. His father was still around, smoking his pipe in the backyard where the tree grew to ten feet. Smoking his pipe and wondering why he felt so happy every evening. And that's why Massimo had the two grooves on his forehead. That's where the spaceship was attached to his head.

When Massimo stopped glowing, we went back to the group. They were taking photos with their iPhones. Some smiled, but mostly they kept their faces at about thirty degrees from the camera. Pretending it wasn't there. Pretending they didn't care, and they wouldn't spend hours obsessing over the photographs after they'd been tagged. Everyone tries the casually disinterested look. I look good from thirty degrees too. And with the crooked smile, or smirk. It was the French-Mauritian or Mauritian-French girl taking photos. Celine. I knew what she'd do—blur out the edges with Instagram, add the scratches, and upload them in a day. Hazy photos of a bygone era. Manufacturing nostalgia. About the good times.

Celine with Maya. Rome 2012, la dolce vita. Like.

Liesbeth lays out a plan for malnutrition in Tanzania. Like.

Me in apartment, scrolling down phone book. No one to call. Like.

Rome, with angel statues and Michelangelo. Like.

Massimo with head split open. Fractured leg, blood dribbling out of penis. Like.

Pooja in canal, slightly stunned. Like.

How many photos can you like in a lifetime? How many can you share? How nostalgic can you get about yesterday? About five minutes ago? These people could be nostalgic about dinner by the time dessert comes.

I was flipping through photographs. Real ones. On paper, in a magazine. I saw Michael Douglas. He had throat cancer. He was in a white linen jacket and a pink shirt, looking all dignified and sexy while he announced it. Throat Cancer could be a fashion line he looked so good saying it. Stage Four from the House of Cancer. Five thousand victims in the US every year. Must be a hundred thousand in India. Throats roasted and lungs fried out of order, like in the pictures on the packets. Eighty percent chance of survival, they said. He had a sore throat for a month.

Holy shit. I had a throat ache. Had one for three weeks. Could feel it every day. I tried to read but the lines were fading away. I blew through the straw into my vodka tonic and it burped back.

I cleared my throat. It hurt. Don't think about it. Don't panic. The lines came back: other symptoms include numbness in the face. I stretched my jaws. Swallowed. No spit, but something was going down. But these were the stories that happened to other people. Alien abductee. Young software billionaire. Young cancer martyr. The good ones always die young. "He was such a good soul, couldn't hurt a fly. But you know, those are the ones God wants back." Somewhere Charlton Heston has a stable full of young men and women.

I tried taking a sip of the vodka. Tried to feel it swirling inside my mouth. Rolling down my throat.

Some girl came to me. What does your name mean? I looked up. Krantik? It means the fighter. Fighting against what? Against oneself, against the universe, I think. Wow, that's so profound. I smiled at her. This could have been my chance. But I didn't have the time. Could I feel my cheeks? I wasn't sure. I pulled Massimo out of the group.

We went outside and he rolled a joint. He could roll in a minute flat. Mix in palm, slap on paper, roll, lick, twist end closed. We were in the alley behind the kitchen. There was a couple kissing in the dark end. We might have looked cool, like figures out of an indie movie. Sometimes I couldn't remember if a video was on YouTube or in my memory. Everything was an image of an image of an image. But that's not why I smoked. I liked it.

Then I remembered. I think I may have throat cancer, I told Massimo.

Don't be stupid, Massimo said.

What do you mean? Have you even noticed: I've had this sore throat for a month. I can't swallow properly.

Have a paracetamol. He wasn't even interested; he looked at the couple. Now they were moving and grinding against each other. I thought I heard the guy fart.

I had to show a doctor. Or maybe I shouldn't. Or maybe I would be a fighter. Shaven head, thirty kilos lighter, but always a brave smile on my face. All the nurses in the cancer institute nursing their mega crushes on me. Krantik. The lion-hearted young man. His story can't end now.

I might be dying, I said to Massimo.

Aren't we all?

I'm serious.

Listen, I have some brandy at home, maybe we could go over after this. Good for your throat too. We went back in.

The party people were all there. They were like the Internet. They were everywhere, I could ask them about anything in the world and they'd have some answer. But I couldn't get to know a thing about myself. I had to leave; I wasn't feeling well. Maybe everything was okay, but then why did I feel a ball of lead in my chest?

I had to get back home. I couldn't spend the rest of my life talking to deer.

PALACONTO

This is happening to a hundred thousand people. 100,000.

You knew it, even before the biopsy came in. You knew, because the floor of your stomach had fallen right through your guts the first time you heard the word and you could feel your ass tighten. You could have pissed yourself, but you just held your wife's hand tighter. And then the doctor told you he had bad news, but it wasn't all that bad. You smiled but you squeezed even harder. Aren't these the moments a life is made up of?

I try to swallow. Feel my cheeks. In the morning, I tried to meditate. One of those methods where you feel your whole body, inch by inch. Move from toe to ankle to that part in the back, the lower leg, what's it called? Damn. Start again.

And then you're standing in front of the mirror and you're crying. You taste the salt in the corner of your lips where it's seeping in. Now your mouth is stupidly curled around and you can barely speak. The brave speeches you will make. You see your wife years later, buying grocery, having a glass of wine, on a balcony and looking into the bloody sky. Is she thinking of you? Or is she being fucked by . . . No. You grip the basin harder, everything is wet. You can't see anymore because the world is melting in your eyes.

This can't be happening to me, you think. Only it is. Or maybe you're chosen. By whom? For what?

Our whole lives we try to build. But actually we are just falling apart.

Colosseo. 76 AD. Cause of ruin: moisture, humidity, earthquake in 1913.

Once maybe you were a child and you scored a home run and you thought life would always be beautiful. If you were in India, you scored the winning runs for your school team and felt the bat tingling in your hand while the ball exploded to the boundary. That was the sweetest sight in the world. But now you're dying. I had spent a week in this beach called Palolem in Goa with a girl I used to know. We woke up and walked down the sand and through the villages, the sun warming our heads and the sound of the sea constantly in our ears. Once we woke up and I had the best prawn sandwich in the world. She was sitting with me and we were both lost. That might be the happiest moment of my life. Have you had a holiday like that? Or do you remember when you had slipped your hand under someone's shirt and felt a breast as soft as a mango? Or down someone's trousers to tame the one-eyed snake. No, I don't really call it that.

Krantik. 1982. Cause of ruin: Tobacco, alcohol, keeping up.

I don't have memories. A few, but I'm never sure. I like to
think I don't. But you, you can't leave your husband behind.
Because now you remember it all. You even remember what
hasn't happened yet. Not the children, can't leave them
either. Tommy's sleeping in his room, curled into a ball. You
can't even look at him, because you might start blubbering
and crash to the floor. And Kathy's not married. Or Rani,
or Ayu, I don't know where you are. She'll have a wedding
photograph, between your husband and her groom; yes, it's
that nice boy who works in consulting. Next to your husband is a flower vase. That could have been you.

I don't even have children. Don't want them. But I could
still miss them.

Pooja. 1983. Cause of ruin: little crucial bits coming undone
inside her head. Whatever it is, it's not about me.

I had a doctor's appointment. I had to go. I walked past the
Roman Forum. 800-100 BC. Sacked by Goths, shifting soil
formations.

I saw this old lady, she had a permanent scowl on her face. I
asked her the way. I said *per favore*. I'm always polite. When
I started learning Italian, I learnt the polite words first: *per
favore, grazie*. I could never figure out the people who learn
the swear words in foreign languages and then laugh about
them over their fourth beer. "Do you know what they call
balls in Spanish? Have you heard the Vietnamese one about

your grand-mom being a whore?" Fuck those dickheads. We need to be civil. If we're not civil, we would just be apes with iPhones. And my *per favore* worked. She thought for a few seconds and then started explaining the route. The one I knew. She wasn't smiling, but she wasn't rude. Just looked melancholic, in a permanent kind of way. I had read about an old lady in the coastal villages of Cinque Terre, up in the north. In the dead of winter, when Italians stayed home with wind in their throats or air in their stomachs or those too-specific ailments Italians are always suffering from, when it was that cold, she'd walk down the main road to the sea with her jacket wide open, the icy wind blowing her hair into a comet behind her. It would take a minute for each step, but she'd keep walking. All the way to the water. Thirty years ago, her husband had died at sea, dragged in by the biggest fish he had ever seen. And now the old lady would walk to the sea and throw meat into the water. Every evening. Prosciutto, sliced thin. Parma ham. Mortadella with little knobs of fat peppered all over. She was feeding her husband. If he wasn't already dead, he'd probably have died of cholesterol. The sea feeder finished giving me directions; the scowl came back to her face.

I also saw a group of girls. Italian with puffed-up jackets; one was wearing beads that hung low across her cleavage. I didn't stop them. It wasn't about the girls. It wasn't about sex. Otherwise I wouldn't have asked the old sea feeder. I would never sleep with her. I mean fuck her, or be fucked by her. Unless she was dying and wanted me to. I don't think I could deny a dying person anything. I'm filled with Christian charity in that way. Maybe I should tell these girls I was dying, might be dying. There was a lump in my throat and it had a life of its own.

I needed to relax. There was no point getting worked up; I was going to a doctor anyway. I tried the walking meditation. Opening my chakras. If you embrace the universe, the universe will embrace you back.

There were flowers that looked like cherry blossoms on the edge of the road. The Japanese kind. Some had opened into little purple stains in the sky. Somewhere in Tokyo, Japanese kids must be photographing them. And then they go home and study for their exams. If they fail, they kill themselves by pushing pencils through their noses. The bridge of the nose breaks and pierces the brain. Instant death. The Japanese have it all figured out. Pooja's obviously not Japanese.

When I walked into the doctor's office, he had a huge chart behind him. Pieces of nose and throat stripped of their skin. A Rolling Stones mouth wide open with pretty white teeth. The doctor's eyelids had rolls, they also had little warts on them. Maybe he had cancer too.

So, young man, what is the problem?

I have a sore throat.

Yes, this is the season. Everyone is getting a sore throat.

I've had it for a month. I think I have problems swallowing.

The weather has been crazy. Climate change. I'll give you a cough syrup, that'll sort everything out. What colour is the sputum? The spit?

I don't know; I haven't seen any. Could you check the inside?

He pressed my tongue down with a spoon and shoved a torch in. He asked me to make that stupid Aaaaeee sound.

Slightly red, but it's okay. Try a salt-water gargle.

No, could you check again. I think there's something in the throat. There could be a growth.

He smiled. It may have been a smirk. Bastard. And then he shoved a pipe with a light at the end down my throat. Nearly choked me; it felt like I was giving a blow job. A blow job to a giant steel robot. With a very thin dick. Maybe he was malnourished. Maybe he was dying; so I had to do it.

All is okay, he said.

I can't feel my cheeks, I said.

Yes, it is cold.

Doctor. I spoke slowly; that's when people take you seriously. I think there might be something wrong. It's not normal to have a sore throat for a month. Also, I can feel some discomfort in my throat. And when I breathe.

Not normal, but it's not abnormal. And this time, he definitely smirked.

He pulled out a thinner pipe and pushed it into a nostril. This may feel uncomfortable, but it'll take only a minute. I started breathing in, breathing out. One nostril. A car with one headlight. What happened to Jakob Dylan? There was a mirror in the room; I saw him peering into my nostril.

This isn't happening. An image of an image. Breathe in.
Out. Yin and yang.

All is okay. I'll give you something to gargle with. If it doesn't
improve in three days, I'll also give you some antibiotics.

Maybe he's right. Embrace the universe. This can't be my
story. I'm not even a minor celebrity.

When I left, they charged me for every pipe he pushed into
me.

I should have gone back to the office. My boss wanted a
project report. He asked me the previous week. The dead-
line is yesterday, he said. Chop chop. Markus; he was Swed-
ish or Finnish or something. Flossed his teeth every day.
Played tennis twice a week. Bowling on Wednesday evenings.
The company can't afford bottlenecks, he said. I'm trying to
make you the sharp end of the machine. If you're a bottle-
neck, we have to do something about it. Is that clear? He
did a thumbs-up, his teeth blazed open at the same time.
Maybe it was automatic. Smile, raise thumb. Chop chop.
Floss. Tennis. Sharp end of the machine.

I hadn't done anything about the report. He'd want my
head on a file. Go to his bowling club with his fingers stuck
in my ears. Perfect Ten.

Maybe I should go back to the office. But I was on sick
leave. And it was the beginning of the rest of my life. I had
just survived throat cancer, the possibility of throat cancer.

We are surviving possibilities all the time. The possibility of being mauled alive by a Chinese panda. Of being roasted on a spit and cannibalised by an Elton John-worshipping cult. In the middle of Manhattan. Things happen.

But I had survived a distinct possibility of impending death. That does not happen all the time. So fuck Markus. I was taking the day off. The Colosseo was crumbling. And some day it will fall. Markus was flossing every day.

I was alive. With my chakras opening into purple blossoms that had the universe in the middle of each ring of petals, the earth with a billion hungry people in the middle of the universe, little cancerous cells growing in the middle of their bodies and either the cells would get them or death would. There was no escape. I was getting morbid again. So I stopped thinking. Maybe it was the steroids up my ass.

No, I wasn't a drug mule, or a Nicaraguan drug-sex-slave. I had haemorrhoids. Piles. The first time it happened, it felt like a bolt of lightning running through my body, upside down. I went to the doctor and he said it was only a pain in the ass.

You mean I just get it from sitting on my ass?

And you get it from your lifestyle, these modern times. This was in India. He loved talking about the glory days of our country: between the fourteenth and fifteenth centuries. No one had haemorrhoids back then. And we invented the zero.

You have a sedentary lifestyle with dietary and lifestyle excesses. Dip your bottom in warm water every two hours.

We had gunpowder in India before the Chinese: did you know that? Don't sit up too long. The pressure from your body settles on the sphincter, he said. What the fuck is the sphincter?

What about some ointment? That's how I got the steroid prescription the first time. Numbs the nerves in the ass. I googled it: Ben Johnson used some variant to win his race.

So Piles and I spent the weekend together. I watched TV sideways from the couch. The doctors on TV had found some girl with four legs and four arms. They had to operate on her. They named her Lakshmi: multi-limbed goddess of wealth. And some white guy had won a Bollywood dance contest. Everyone claimed it was unfair, what would he know about Bollywood? But he had learnt his steps from Farah Khan, the goddess of hip thrusting. She was just four-limbed. I drank two litres of juice. Had to piss all the time. Missed the pot a lot—I was hobbling because of the ass. So I started using the juice bottles on the couch. The empty juice bottles.

Things got better. They always do. First they happen; then they get better. Things would get better for Markus too. As long as he kept flossing. What he didn't know was—floss enough times and you will certainly end up dead. Flossing till the end of his life was the surest way of meeting death. It would get better for Pooja too. She'd meet some guy her parents found for her. They'd have sex. Only missionary style. She'd scream, but not too loudly, because then what kind of woman would her husband think she was. And she'd want him to go down, but of course she would never tell him. He had such a perfect life with his corner office in the bank and his ties with solid lines and the one with the ethnic patterns that he'd wear on Fridays. How could he go down with a tie like that? Maybe he'd want to go down as well; but then how could he say so to a nice girl like that. And they'd have kids—three, the two girls and then the boy because they didn't stop trying till the boy came—and foreign trips. Going up the Eiffel Tower. Taking the elevator down. Just when it has its first ever accident and they free-fall for ten seconds when their faces are frozen in the horror of realising that all of it meant nothing and then they'd end up dead in a soup of twisted metal with one rod spiked through his ethnic pattern. On his scarf, he wouldn't be wearing a tie on holiday, but he got a scarf with ethnic patterns too. Okay, I didn't wish that last part: the part about the lift, not the scarf. I didn't wish her ill. I was the greater person.

Anyway, the ass got better. But I got the steroids to Rome. If I feel a little sore, I just stuff some up my ass. It wasn't very comfortable walking with the steroids squishing inside me. So I waited for the bus. And of course it didn't come. In Rome, the bus always comes later than you expect. I should prepare a survival guide for the transport in Rome. I'd even send it to Pooja and her future-solid-tie-husband. How to survive the transport in Rome. The bus always takes longer than you expect. Always. If you plan for the delay, the bus driver will know telepathically, arrive with further delay and still ruin your postponed plans.

I climbed down to the metro. Which was also late. Obviously. The metro takes longer than you expect. If it arrives on time, the metro driver will know your plans telepathically and will stop the metro in between stops for undefined

reasons. Your postponed plans will still be ruined. The
metro really took my trip.

I didn't have plans. But they were still ruined. Then the
old man seated next to me on the bench started talking. I
couldn't understand a word. He spoke fast in Italian and
swallowed the end of every word. I kept saying *davvero*. Sure,
sure. You never know what these old people go on about.
Probably ranting about how things never work. Or about
kids nowadays. People talk all the time in Rome, which is
annoying. Maybe it's good for the community. If you take
the train to another city, the old couple next to you will
ask your name. They will also ask about your job, your
income, your rent and why you missed your cousin's wedding. This is not an intrusion. This is part of building a
community. Also, if you're on the metro, you'll have the
person next to you read your book over your shoulder. Reci-
procity is assured. When the girl next to you is breaking
up, you can read her text messages. This is not an intrusion. This is the free flow of knowledge. Also, it means you
can look at her boobs and pretend you're just reading her
messages.

Maybe the old guy, the word-swallower, was trying to
seduce me. Who knows with these old people? Maybe he
was a priest. I wasn't much older than a kid myself. No,
I shouldn't judge people. We hear all kinds of shit about
everyone. One can't believe most of that. But the bit about
priests getting off on kids is probably true. The word-eater
leaned in and said something with a cackle. Spit looped out
from between his missing teeth. I said *davvero* once more
and walked away.

I didn't have anywhere to go. So I asked a guy. Ciao. Colos-seo? A shrug of the shoulders: rejection. I could see the monument in the distance, so obviously he knew. Maybe he didn't want to talk. He was gnawing on his lower lip and looking away. Maybe he'd been caught fucking his neigh-bour's wife. Or his neighbour's dog. In which case, he prob-ably didn't have much to say. Or maybe he was a priest in a leather jacket.

But I didn't have to worry about him. I had cherry blos-soms and opening chakras and Massimo and a stash of weed at home. I even had the Colosseo. Maybe I'd take a few photographs. I walked away from the metro. Sometimes walking is the best thing you could do in Rome—the whole place might be falling apart but it's happening with such unbearable grace. This city has been around forever. And there have always been ruins. Here, people are used to the beauty of things falling apart. I shouldn't take it for granted. It might be a toilet bowl, but it is one fit for Winona Ryder. Even for Morgan Freeman.

Maybe God doesn't look like either of them. We humans have been around for what, a couple of million years? But the cockroaches—I remember reading, I read a lot—have been in pretty much the same shape for over a hundred million years. As ugly, scurrying around and even flying into our faces in summer, being crushed into red veins and white goo under dinosaur feet. But they've made it this far. There must be a reason. It's probably because God is not Jesus with his Jim Morrison beard and Kurt Cobain eyes and God is not Invisible Man Allah who was too shy to be painted or photographed and God is not Vishnu with his Smurf-blue face as handsome as that TV actor—no one remembers his name now—dancing on the ten-hooded serpent. God was the cockroach in the kitchen when the last supper was being prepared. I didn't have to worry. I was okay as long as I didn't use the Doom spray in the kitchen too often.

I shouldn't blaspheme, I thought. I didn't want lightning to strike me down on a clear day like this. The steroids in my ass could be a conductor. I should check—that could be really dangerous.

Then I saw the girl: she was leaning against the door of the gelato place near the bus stop. She held a cigarette in her left hand, the whole hand was closed around the filter and the cigarette was pointing away, as if she had a burning claw. Behind her, faces were pasted on the gelato counter while the server scooped into cups in a row: *mandorle, pistachio, fior di latte, cannella con cioccolato.* I looked at the flavours. And I saw her looking at me. I was normally like the cockroach God, too small and insignificant till you step on me and I spill my mess all over your floor. I'm usually that insignificant. But she was looking at me. So I asked her.

Excuse me, I said in English. She raised one eyebrow into a question. Only one. While the other eyebrow didn't move. I had never seen anyone do that: it was like a miracle.

I wanted to pose a difficult question, one that would take some time. Do you know the way to Gianicolo?

She stubbed her cigarette in the gelato in her right hand and I could smell the puff of tiramisu gelato smoke. Okay, she said.

Okay?

I'm going to Gianicolo too, she said. Let me show you the way. Should we walk?

Yes, we could walk.

And so my question that wasn't a question had found an answer.

She walked a fraction faster than me, so I had to keep up with longer steps till I could feel the unnamed back of my leg.

Where are you from?

India. But I don't go back often.

Why not?

Because there is no one I want to meet.

One billion people and no one to meet?

Not really. My mother's there, but we Skype often. Have you ever been to India?

No, she said. Only saw lots of Indians in London. I was there for five years.

How was that?

The most crowded place in the world. And the loneliest.

I know about that. I was there too.

We had reached the Lungotevere by the river. People spilled
out from the bars with their wine glasses, their feet hoisted
against the bar walls, blowing long plumes of smoke into
the early evening. When we were crossing the bridge, she
stopped in the middle to light a cigarette and lean against
the railing. I stopped too. I had to say something smart. But
I couldn't think of anything, so I kept quiet. Tried to keep
a cigarette dangling from the edge of my lips. I'm an image
of an image. But then I stopped trying. I was walking with
this girl. I couldn't believe it. I mean this was not unbeliev-
able in the alien-abduction anal-probe league. But maybe
alien-waving-from-the-TV league. Which is not as unbeliev-
able as it seems. Okay, stay in the moment.

An older woman walked past us, leading a little dog on a
leash. The girl sneered. The old woman used to be a talk
show host on one of the Berlusconi TV channels, the girl
said.

Berlusconi owns TV channels?

He owns everything. He wants to own the whole fucking
world.

I had a plan for owning the world, I said. She wanted to
know more, so I told her. I'd start a website, and ask people
to pay me one euro each. Whatever for? Just pay me a euro,
nothing in return. I get enough money and soon I'll be a
millionaire. But I'd be a millionaire thanks to all the people
who paid me. So I'd live the millionaire lifestyle like they
wanted. I would have the money, but I'd spend it however

my donors wanted me to. Why would they want you to be a millionaire? Because they'll never make it. The whole world wants them to believe they will. That they'll drive a sleek car, the car will come with a blonde attached to it, the blonde comes with invitations to the coolest parties, the coolest parties have rock stars and people who lounge in Mediterranean villas with pools that stretch to the sea, and someday they'll all be part of it. All this will come true, only if they used this razor. What are you talking about? I'll live the life for them, the one they have been promised. They can even tell me what to do, tell me how to spend the money. I'll let them decide. If they wanted a Bottega Veneto bag—Veneta not Veneto—yes, that one, if they want one, then I'll own one. If they want a yacht, I'll buy a yacht. On a lake of Prosecco. And I'll upload pictures and tweets only for the people who paid me. They'll finally live the good life. Not the whole thing, but in little doses. They'll live it through me. But we are all living different lives, aren't we? All they have to do is donate one euro on my website. Just once.

I don't think it'll ever work. It'll only make people more miserable.

I offer them the millionaire lifestyle for just a euro and they'll say no?

But they're not living it. You are.

They're living enough of it. I'm spending the money like they want me to. They'll have all the updates, all the digital information. That's as good as the real thing. Maybe everyone will invest in my "I want to be a millionaire" fund, and then they can all take it easy while I live out their dreams.

No more pressure. I'll offer green points too. I may become a millionaire, or billionaire, but if you ask me, I'll only fly economy for a month. Okay, a week.

What if they ask you to give it away to charity?

They won't do that.

How can you be so sure?

If we helped all the poor, screwed-up people below us, where would that leave us? That would leave us at the bottom.

What if they ask you to organize a spectacular suicide?

You think they might do that?

I think that might be the first thing they would ask when you become famous. Celebrities die to keep the rest of us alive.

But if I did it, would it make me a fool or a martyr?

Is there a difference?

Below us, the trees along the Tevere River shook in the wind, their branches bristling with plastic bags. When the river floods, all the plastic from upstream gets stuck in the branches. A tree even had a child's tricycle once, twenty feet in the sky.

What about you? You don't have a plan? I asked her.

I do. I think I'd like to start a revolution.

Not again.

This will change everything.

What will you fight for?

Palaconto.

What's that? My Italian's not too good.

Palaconto.

What does that mean?

Nothing. It's a nothing-word. Which means it could be an everything-word.

Why would people support you?

Because palaconto could mean whatever they want it to mean. It means we don't want the global capitalist aristocracy we have inherited. We don't want democracy. We don't want the media and advertising manipulation of our thoughts and desires. We don't want Elvis. And we don't want Che. All we want is palaconto. Palaconto for me. Palacontiamo for all of us. Palaconti for you.

It's a revolution you can conjugate, I said.

Yes, the first ever.

And if you don't know what it means? Can you still join?

You can only join the revolution if you know what it means.

But it doesn't mean anything.

Or whatever you want it to. You can graffiti the walls with it. Giant letters on each metro cabin. The crowd scream-ing palaconto in a Roma-Lazio match. A projector in the middle of the Colosseo painting palaconto on the skies. Computers and banks and government departments crash-ing because of the palaconto virus.

How many people do you think would join you?

I don't know. Millions. Anyone who knows what it means.

Would they have a euro to spare for my website?

She laughed. Not in a smirking, sophisticated way. She laughed with her mouth split in comic-book glee. I could even see a cavity in her lower row. Her name was Chiara. Clear. Clear as the morning sky, I suppose her parents had thought. Also means light beer. She had finished her mas-ter's in London, worked there for a few years—this and that, mostly that—and then finished a PhD. And now she had a research job. Nine to five, the usual grind. Slave to the bureaucracy, pretending to be an intellectual, she said.

Should we continue? she asked.

Where?

Aren't you going to Gianicolo?

Yes, I am.

We started walking uphill. I felt the back of my legs, crying out to be named. How could she walk up so easily? Maybe she was also a trained assassin—she was wearing black. And her clothes were snug (I was looking). Aerodynamic. Helps to leap across buildings or onto train roofs. I didn't even know the girl. I didn't really know Pooja either. Forget Pooja. Fuck Pooja. I mean, pull-out-last-minute Pooja.

Are you here alone? she asked.

Yes, in Rome. I mean, now I have a few friends. What about you?

I stay alone. I have a banker boyfriend. Sort of.

Is he a sort of banker? Or a sort of boyfriend?

He's definitely a banker.

We reached a bend on the road. We were halfway up the hill. Rome was spread in front of us. Domes and towers across the city punctured the sky. I could see the two sculpted chariots on top of the Vittoriano. The winged ladies riding the chariots looked like they were hovering in midair. We sat down on the edge of the road. Chiara scanned the horizon, as if she was looking for something. The ruins in front of us were washed in the dying light. Her arm grazed against mine. When she looked away, her arm pressed into mine through her jacket.

You weren't really coming to Gianicolo, were you?

What?

You weren't looking for Gianicolo. I saw you ask the guy at the bus stop for Colosseo.

I couldn't reply. So I tried looking harder at the chariot. The winged lady had a sword in her hand.

And you know, she said, I wasn't coming to Gianicolo either.

But now we're both here, I said.

She pointed to the Vatican dome. Behind us cars swept the edge of the road and snatches of stereo music floated to us. We sat looking at the city, at the undeniable beauty of things falling apart.

She took off her jacket. That's when I saw the cuts on her arm. Below her wrists, lines all in a row, a few deeper and redder. And then a whole rash of cuts, running helter-skelter across her forearms.

I wanted to take those little lines. Rearrange them into something else. Make sense of them. Make a word. Maybe Palaconto.

HERE COMES THE SUN

Pain will make you feel alive. They say you should stay still when it comes.

But I can't. I'm in the loo, and my old friend is back. My ass splits open and the world is being turned inside out. I hold on to the wall, I'm shaking so much. This is like Genesis, the universe cracking open from nothing.

When I'm done, I look down. The toilet bowl is a gentle red with my blood. Like a Monet painting. I'm still trembling. After I wash up, the blood is gone. Only the triumphant turd remains sunk in the water. Now it's a Damien Hirst installation.

I was back home. I mean India. My sister had called a few times. Then she mailed and said it was a "Family Crisis" and I had to return for a few days. Yes, she capitalized the words. If she had used CAPS LOCK, I would have asked

41

about her husband. Ex-husband. Who's now bonking a TV actress. A B-grade one. We don't talk about it.

I couldn't avoid meeting my mother for lunch. She made vegetable curry, some tubes with seeds. I never know what she uses, mostly because I don't care. I cook, but I don't bother other people for their recipes. I don't particularly care for Indian food either. Don't ask me about that stuff, find someone else. They'll tell you about Indian mother's spices and mangoes and elephant dung and shit.

You should have handled it better, Ma said.

I didn't jump. She did, I said.

You've ruined that poor girl's life. What will I tell Pooja's parents?

I kept my eyes fixed on the TV. The TV used to be the eye of God. Now it's Facebook. I obey.

Are you listening?

Yes, Ma.

I love you.

I know.

If he were still alive, he would have been heartbroken by all this.

When my mom uses the unspecified He, she's talking about my father. He's dead. Extinguished. He was great, sang

Dylan to me. I miss him sometimes. My dad, not Dylan (who's still around in some form). Dylan was cool till he did the advertisement for Victoria's Secret. He was ultra-fucking cool. Have you seen the Dylan documentary, *No Direction Home*? I think that's a great name. If I ever wrote a book about my time in Rome, I think I'd call it *No Direction Rome*.

Anyway, my ass is still sore. But I'm not grumpy. I'm the Dalai Lama around my mom. That's the least I can do.

Yes, Ma. But I'm working hard. And the job is going well, I said. I didn't know what else to say.

Have you called her?

I tried.

And then she was crying. So I told her the vegetables were really nice.

I went for a walk when she was asleep. People passed me on the streets. I didn't ask anyone for directions. A mother dragged her child, back from school. His shirt was stained with ink and he was really upset about it. On a corner, a man juggled between his briefcase, a cigarette in the process of being lit, and his mobile phone. Buy the Tata stocks, sell Yahoo, hold on to Reliance till it reaches 500. Fill me with numbers because I have run out of words.

We have all seen the same things: pools filling with litter, cars looking for their next prey on the roads, lions yawning into the sun (only on TV), skies clouding up and being sliced by planes that take us farther away from wherever we are. If you're a plane technician and you're checking the engines, don't ever stand in front of the propeller that's still running. Then before you can say "Wheels okay," you would get sucked in ass first at supersonic speed into the waiting blades that will blend you. Later, the gleaming metal ring around the fan will be lined with your intestines. Will they have a speech at your funeral? The bravest among us, some will say. The best go first. Peace be upon him.

Peace only comes from knowing. Not from dying. Though I'm not sure. If I meet the Buddha on the road, I'll send him a friend request.

As long as office lights switch on and off and Excel files vomit numbers into unending sheets and I wait for footsteps in my office corner, I will have to go on. Nothing ever really ends. Or it takes too damn long.

So I called Chiara again. It was the twelfth call in the last three days. If I didn't include the four times I hung up before the phone rang. She didn't pick up. Again. So I went home and started packing.

If you were on a boat on a still lake and leaned over to embrace the moon, would you risk death for it? If you had two hours to live, what could your message to the world (your last Facebook update) be? Gangnam style? A LOLcat on Gangnam? Or one of those pathetic animal torture videos: cat on a string, half-skinned, between two smiling teenagers?

Are you leaving? It's just been two days. It was my mother.

I have a meeting day after tomorrow. I just remembered.

But your underwear's still drying.

I'll be wearing a suit. No one will notice.

I worry for you.

I don't, I said. And then I said I was sorry. She didn't
ask why. She was leaning against the doorframe. Maybe I
should have held her. But then I would have to step over
the suitcase and all my clothes scattered over its open jaws.
I tapped her shoulder instead.

On the plane, I dreamt of Chiara. Or maybe I thought of
her because I was aware of what was happening. In my
Technicolor thought sphere, she didn't accept me. In fact
she was so annoyed with my unending stalker calls that she
came to my flat and called me a creepy worm. I couldn't
see her next move because my head was bowed down. She
whipped out an uppercut on my jaw and before I could collapse she knee-slammed me against the wall. Then she left
the door open for her boyfriend. Who I discovered wasn't
a geeky banker type slouched over his financial calculations.
He was the cutthroat silver-tongued sort who owned a yacht
on the Mediterranean. Also did one-armed push-ups on the
deck for fun. Just before his glistening six-pack body knifed
into the crystal water to wrestle with sharks. In my apartment, he beat me into a whimpering pulp. Show me your

arms. Get up and fight, motherfucker. But I refused. I was curled on the floor.

It was cold inside the plane. And it was getting awkward: unadulterated misery sometimes gives me a hard-on. I tried to ball my knees into my stomach. One of the stewardesses brought a blanket and because I pretended to be asleep, she laid it over me. That was sweet. I could have married her. Not for the sex. I could have also paid off all her debts, or her children's college education even if I had to slave myself out. If she had asked me right then.

How are you? Had a good flight?

Okay.

On holiday here?

No, I work here.

Dove lavori? The taxi driver turned the mirror to see me, but I could barely see his eyes, hidden behind his grey frizzled hair.

Non parlo Italiano bene.

No problem, no problem. We all speak English now.

We have to, I said. We were driving past the Roman aqueducts that delivered water to the city. Now they were mostly gone, but some long stretches of the giant elevated canals rose into the sky beside us, like ramps for alien ships.

Why do I have to?

Because I speak only English.

So if you pay me, I have to do whatever you want? I still couldn't see his eyes, but I knew he was looking at me.

No. That's not what I meant. I mean it's so common. And I don't speak any other European language. I was stating a fact, not a demand.

Your command is my wish, he said. You are the guest here.

In Italy?

No, in my car.

Thank you.

Niente. Niente, signor. He raised the volume on his stereo. You like jazz?

I don't really listen to jazz.

John Coltrane. 'My Favorite Things.' You know what one of my favorite things is?

Pizza? And I hoped at once it didn't sound sarcastic. A few headlights from cars on the other lane scooped out bits of the night. The roads had no streetlights.

One of my favourite things is meeting people like you.

Same here. I like meeting Italians.

I'm not full Italian. Twenty years in California. My English sounds Italian to you?

No, it sounds great.

Good, we need to understand each other perfectly.

Yes, different communities should talk to each other.

Not communities. You and me. One hand raised and tilting the mirror, the other tapping the steering wheel, slightly offbeat.

Yes, of course.

Are you a community?

No, I said. I put on my seat belt. Maybe I'm a part of one. Or of many.

Are you a highway?

What?

Are you a road? Do you know where you're going?

I held on to the handrest. His feet were on the accelerator now. But his gaze was on the mirror. We swung around a curve.

Raindrops on roses. Whiskers on kittens. He was singing. Girls in white dresses with blue satin sashes. You like them?

Could you slow down a little? Please.

LONG FLIGHTS AND TAXIS. RECEIPTS FOR PAYMENTS, he shouted. These are some of your favorite things. Aren't they, Signor?

I don't need a receipt.

Today is your lucky day. You know why?

No. Sir, I can get off here.

You can get out anytime you like. This is not Hotel California. His foot pressed further on the accelerator. We zipped past a red light and other waiting cars.

Then you can stop here. I couldn't move. I just tried looking for his eyes in the mirror.

But this car's not stopping, not tonight, he said. You didn't ask why you're so lucky?

Why?

Because you're the last person to talk to me. Fifty-seven years screwing around and I end my life with you. His eyes weren't red, they were aluminum grey. The wheels were scorching tarmac. Coltrane couldn't keep up with us.

When we got to the GRA highway, he explained like a doctor studying my haemorrhoids: I'll drive off the bridge.

Imagine, this taxi flying through the skies and crashing on the rails below. You like that?

I wanted to get out of there. But I also wanted skies filled with planes, like a tangerine dream of industrial smog. I wanted the Colosseo torn down and replaced by black gleaming video game arcades. I wanted African genocide in Europe with Berlusconi whoring out every woman and then moving on to her shocked brothers.

You can jump out if you want. I'll slow down and you could jump, he offered.

But I couldn't tell him what I wanted. So I kept quiet and stayed still.

What do you want to do? I unbuckled my seat belt. I wanted a world made of celluloid-Instagram mountains and cats being choked on strings.

The GRA flew up to us. He needled the car to the right, the taxi slammed against the border railing and I was flung against the opposite door. Everything was jerking violently and I was plastered to the back of the seat. Then the car battered to a stop and I was folded on the floor.

Hey, the driver leaned over, and through the shower of his hair I saw blood slithering out of his mouth. Hey. I waited for the bones in my body to stop jangling.

Which is your favourite Beatle? he asked me.

George Harrison.

Great stuff. I heard his CD player clicking and then the guitars rolled gently into "Here Comes the Sun."

When we got to the hospital, he dug me out of the back and carried me into the emergency section though I might have managed to walk on my own. But I couldn't move my right leg without being washed over in pain. And from the salt in my mouth, I knew a couple of teeth were coming loose.

You knew I was joking, right?

About what?

About driving off the bridge?

I wasn't sure. It would have been quite a sight.

My name is Federico. Fede for short: it means faith.

I'm Krantik. Don't ask me what it means.

Why would I do that?

When I got back home (Fede gave me a free ride), so stuffed with painkillers I couldn't even feel my ass, the stench of dried scrambled eggs on the frying pan welcomed me.

I texted Chiara.

You're not answering my calls because you don't know me.

And I want to see you. Because I don't know you.

There was no reply. I sent one more.

Did you know that if you die of rabies, on the last day you have the most astonishing automatic orgasms of your life? Up to thirty times in a day.

And then the phone rang.

Why are you texting me random shit?

What else do you want me to say?

Come to Via Galvani, the corner with Via Marmorata.

I half-limped, half-crawled (I exaggerate, but only a little) there in twenty minutes.

What the hell? You're bleeding?

Yes, I said. And I'm broken. But there's nothing to protect inside, so it's okay.

She held my hand and dragged me to the giant nineteenth-century doors of her building. Before she had turned the key, I pressed against her and kissed her. I sucked so hard I could feel my tooth unhinging a little more.

SWEET SPOT

Have you ever felt a sweet spot? The kind you remember, not just as a recorded memory, but as a vibration. You strike a cricket ball or a baseball just right. Feel the tingling bat talk straight to your heart. The ball looping through the air, the bat swinging in your hand, your stretched arms, your waiting body, the ground beneath your feet (sounds dramatic, but that's how it feels), everything is perfectly aligned. Everything is moving, but perfectly still. Or you're playing football (I don't call it soccer, never could) and take a free kick. You have the top right corner of the goal in your head. You drive your lower foot through the ball. It scythes through the air, a silver spoon in clear soup. Beyond the goalkeeper's flailing arms, your ball arrows into the net.

Everything is just as it should be. And you know you've hit the sweet spot. Doesn't happen often, but when it does you know it.

But you're not interested in my knowledge of sports. You only want to know what happened, don't you? I mean about the sex. Did we? Did we not? I don't like talking about that: I'm very private that way. I mean, it's messed up enough, my life, without you meddling around. And why's that always the first question: did you?

But yes. Yes and no.

We were at it. On her single bed. I was looking at her from below, she was looking away. I could see little lines popping up on her brow, above the bridge of her nose. But when I moved up from her gently tingling breasts, she turned and kissed me, our lips sloppy and smacking into each other. I pulled my pants down, and my underwear was still drying in India.

And then she said Stop.

So I stopped. Still throbbing like a dog on heat, but I stopped.

She threw her arms around my back. Pulled me closer till we were cheek to cheek. Rubbed her hands down my back. The lines on her wrists melting into me. I was limp now.

Hold me, she said.

I moved my arms below her neck, till her head was raised. In midair, between locked arms, we waited.

I don't know if sex brings us together. Either Hugh Hefner-style, all one big happy family. Or Bible-style, seed of the lamb and go forth and multiply for the Lord will provide. I don't feel any closer to anyone or anything with sex. If I'm in you (or if you're in me: that hasn't happened yet, but you never know), I don't even remember who I am. How am I supposed to love you? Or even particularly care? Sometimes, when I'm alone in bed, I think of all the people in the world who're having sex right now. And how they all think everything's going to be great just because they're about to come.

Maybe that's why Chiara stopped me. I could hear her breathing. In. Out. And then I was breathing with her.

That was my sweet spot.

In a Virginia suburb, a fifty-year-old is thrusting into his wife. He wants to get it over with soon, because there's the meeting with Steve from head office early in the morning. She's thinking about blueberry muffins.

Chiara and me? We were just waiting. Breathing.

Or in Egypt, a young girl has sneaked her boyfriend in for the night. While he goes down on her, she's moaning, but she also remembers all the angry hot men she saw during the revolution. He remembers his last koshari meal, with extra onions and chickpeas, because that's what it smells like down there.

Just hold me, Chiara said.

Sure.

There was a little blood from my still-aching mouth on her breast. I wiped it off.

You don't have to do anything. Just hold me.

What are you thinking of? I asked her.

Nothing. And you?

Gelato. I made up the answer, but since I made it up, I guess I was thinking of it.

Which flavour?

Anguria. Or cannella.

Then let's go.

Where?

I know a place that's still open.

Seriously? You want gelato now?

No, you want gelato. You're the one thinking about it.

I'm just thinking, like randomly.

So, let's go. Or are you going to be upset because we didn't have sex and we'll be having gelato instead?

Why would I be offended?

You know, the male infantile super-ego thing. But I just wanted to be with you for a while, not . . .

I didn't want to have sex either.

Then why did you pull your pants down?

Yours were down too. I was following the dress code.

Okay, then put them on. The dress code just changed, she said.

We were still cheek to cheek, breath to breath. Then I got up and put on my trousers.

We took a night bus and then walked towards Santa Maria Maggiore. I dragged my right leg behind us. On our side of the road, a church that stretched for half the block was being restored. They erected a faux-front over the repair, so you only see the rich mauve and beige structure and a glorious sunny day painted on canvas. Even in the middle of the night. But we were walking below the scaffolding, and could see behind—we could see the real walls peeling off.

You know, if we don't meet again, I think I might remember this forever, I said.

What? Us making out?

No. Just you and me walking here.

You'd only remember it if we didn't meet again?

I might remember it if we do meet again. But the memory of a moment can be perfect. Not the memory of years.

What other perfect memory do you have?

I know one. My dad singing Dylan to me: 'Blowing in the Wind.' I remember his fingers strumming the strings.

And you didn't see him much after?

I was a kid. He died. So he remained incomplete. Perfect.

In front of a park, a group of Bangladeshis were sitting around and chatting. The immigrant smell of illegal piss and legal alcohol wafted from the corner.

Aren't you going to ask for directions? Chiara asked me.

No, you know the way.

But you don't know where we're going.

I don't need to know where I'm going. I only want to know where I am.

You're weird.

I'm weird? You're the one who has a huge blowup picture of a pussy above her bed.

It's the origin of the world.

What is?

The painting, that's what it's called: *The Origin of the World*.

That's so self-obsessed.

Just because it's a woman's vagina?

No. Just because we came from there doesn't mean it's the origin of the whole world. That's so anthropocentric. And we didn't come from there. We sort of passed through. It should be called Route of the Human Species, or Inevitable Thoroughfare in the Origin of One Specimen of the Human Species.

You're scared of vaginas, aren't you?

How old are you? Like 107 years? Why're you still talking all Freudian.

Don't be patronizing.

I'm not being patronizing. I'm just being a dick.

We're almost there.

Where?

Gelato. In that bar, they have a counter.

Bar L'Esquilino. It was filled with Italians. In such places, I don't talk much. I don't want to be the stupid foreigner who never learnt Italian. I want to be the taciturn guy who doesn't say much. And I'm not a stupid foreigner anyway, I'm the overpaid expat who doesn't need to learn their language. I speak English. We should all stop learning other languages—Darwinism and efficiency of operation and all. Learn fucking English or don't say anything. There's not much to say anyway.

Should we go in?

Sure. And then I saw Leonardo, so I stopped.

Hold on, I said.

What?

That guy. I pointed to Leonardo. His neck was craned up to the TV. He was still in uniform, and his hand moved blindly from peanut bowl to mouth.

The old man?

Yes, he's my landlord.

So?

He's supposed to be in Brazil. He has a flight to Brazil every two days. Works for Alitalia.

Maybe he missed his flight.

He's the pilot. Can't you see? There is no flight if he's not on it.

Do you want gelato or not?

Can we go get a drink instead? Somewhere else.

Sure. If you have issues with your landlord, we can stay away.

I looked back while we were walking away. Leonardo hadn't moved in a minute. His eyes were glued to the TV. And it was only showing commercials. The crowd swirled around him. Cheeks kissing, people saying the same things to each other every evening: *Ciao, che bella, non mi credo*, did you see Balotelli and his bicycle kick? And Leonardo is watching commercials.

Are you okay? Chiara asked me.

He should be in Brazil, I said. I liked Leonardo: he kept calling me to his terrace and offering wine. Not in an over-familiar way, in a we're both nice guys, so let's hang out way. He's almost sixty, but it doesn't matter. After twenty-two, I don't think I've ever felt older. I thought there would be a time when I'd wake up and know I was grown up. I'm still waiting. Maybe the whole system's delaying adulthood. Buy a Wii, get the new iPhone, get Fruit Ninja installed. Stay young and unsatisfied and you can buy all the shit there is to buy. Is it just our generation? My parents were adults in their twenties. They were ancient when they turned thirty.

My dad smoked a pipe. And started sentences with 'In my days . . .' But Leonardo was different. He didn't feel any older than me. He loved his wine and his coffee. He said he loved Rome the moment he saw her (which is when he was born) and wouldn't give up the city for anything. He also liked to sit on the terrace and watch his turtles fuck. He had nine of them. I grew up with them, he would say, started with three, a mother and her two kids. And now they're almost a football team. Mom fucked one of her kids, and then the family kept at it. They're like hillbillies. Or royalty. Fed them every day of my life. And they don't even know who I am. They don't care. Maybe that's why I love them. Leonardo would sit there with his Chianti and watch them all evening. That's when he was in town. He said he had his flight three times a week. But I saw him in his uniform most days. Office work, management meeting, he explained, sometimes pilots have to stay on the ground.

He should be in Brazil, I said to Chiara again.

We got to a bar. I didn't get gelato. But I wasn't thinking of it anyway, it was just a word that came up. Maybe I was thinking of the word, but not of the actual gelato. If I was thinking of the actual gelato, I wouldn't be thinking of the word. She got a vodka tonic. I got a vino spritz: orange and bubbly. I liked it.

Are you married? Chiara asked me.

Why're you asking me? Does it matter?

No, it doesn't.

No, I'm not.

Do you have any questions for me?

I do, actually. Leonardo has nine turtles on his terrace, I said.

And?

I keep wondering: what do the turtles think about when they have sex?

What do Leonardo's Turtles Think About?

When Federico called me the next day, I should have been surprised. But I was crouching over the toilet bowl examining the mucus that had slithered out with my shit. Mucus is not a good sign: it's supposed to stay inside the body. Stage I: five-year survival rate of 74 percent. Everyone's in with a chance.

Hello? Krantik?

Yes. It's me.

How're you doing? This is Federico.

I know. I'm okay. Great.

It may be Crohn's disease, which isn't fatal. Maybe in the long run. But then everything is fatal in the long run.

Do you want to come and watch the game?

What game? I don't watch much football.

Relax, deep breath, be aware of body and of the universe flowing through chakras. This can be dealt with. Have I been losing weight? Or putting on weight? Why do I keep smoking? Don't do this. Don't self-diagnose. Go to a doctor. If you have inflammatory bowel syndrome, you're at heightened risk. I've always had IBS.

You're in Italy. There's no greater religious experience than watching a Roma-Lazio game. That was Federico's voice.

Maybe it's not mucus at all. The world is filled with light. If I imagine a blue light in front of my eyes, it can heal everything. It's not mucus! It's just the steroid cream, and I've been using too much. What does mucus feel like? I look for some plastic to wrap around my hand.

Hello? Are you there?

Yes, sorry. I was working on something.

I'll get you a beer. Come over. I'll teach you how to be Italian.

I know how to watch a game of football. That's not being Italian. That's being a passive consumer of a spectacle brought to you by the monster advertising industry that endows superficial meaning to the sight of twenty-two men chasing a piece of leather.

You've read too much post-modern analysis to enjoy anything anymore. Just come for a beer!

If there's a bowel obstruction, then I'm in deep shit. I never feel like I've emptied out totally. There's always a little knot of stuff left. There is an overhang in my belly. Stage III B: survival rate of 46 percent.

So are you coming? We're meeting at a bar near your place.

No story that started with "I was having a drink with a psychopathic taxi driver . . ." can ever end well. But a story that starts with "I was bent over the toilet bowl looking at my mucus-covered-shit . . ." can't get any worse. I needed some air.

Yes, hold on. I took off the plastic bag. Give me the address.

I should be rooting for Roma since the city is such a magnificent host. And Federico knew my address; I didn't want to piss him off.

Of course, the bar wasn't close to my place. It was a twenty-minute walk away. I had to stop thinking about my bowel, time to get my head out of my ass. Below my building, I could hear voices and, from above, music from the terrace. Maybe Leonardo had guests over. The turtles must be terrified, all the new faces. Those poor buggers have never left the terrace. And they could live for a hundred years. Either they were all having great sex or some crazy conversation. Maybe Turtles 8 and 9, the youngest ones, were still figuring things out.

Turtle 8: Hey, guess what we have for lunch? Lettuce; slightly rotten.

Turtle 9: Yeah, this is amazing. Who would have thought?

Turtle 8: But we had it yesterday as well. And the day before.

Turtle 9: I know. Who would have thought?

Have you ever wondered about the giant who brings in the food? You know Big Man in Shiny Suit (Leonardo wears his pilot uniform on the terrace most of the time).

Don't spell out his name. That's a sin. You can say BMISS.

Why can't I use his name, if that is his name?

Don't ask me. Turtle 5 told me.

I had asked Turtle 4 last night; she didn't say anything about not spelling his name. She says he is not a name, he is a concept: he is the universe looking after us.

Wait a minute . . . you were with Turtle 4 last night?

Yes. Why?

You're not ready for her. She's a fast one. You're a twat. Has anyone told you that?

I thought I was a turtle.

And don't use that word. We call ourselves Made In His Image. Say MIHI when you talk about yourself.

Whose image?

The food source, our sustainer, our creator. BMISS.

We're made in his image? What does that mean? He doesn't look anything like us.

Have you ever seen his face?

No, it's too high up.

So? He made us. And of course, because we are perfect and at the centre of the universe, he made us as perfect as he possibly could.

We're at the centre of the universe?

You're just too stupid to understand the world. You need to sit down with Turtle 3 for a good long while and figure things out.

How does Turtle 3 know everything?

He was here from the beginning. And he can understand BMISS.

But he's just a turtle.

No. He's a MIHI.

How could he possibly understand BMISS?

Don't ever, ever ask him that; he heard the original Words.

What Words?

Stop bugging me. Let's go look for some worms.

(While they're waddling away to the left corner of the terrace) What does Turtle 3 have to say?

He thinks there's only one giant who matters. BMISS.

But Turtle 2 said there are many giants. I've seen them.

Okay. Let me get this clear: Turtle 3 says there's just one who matters, after all only BMISS feeds us. Turtle 2 says they all play a part. I don't know. But I believe Turtle 3.

Okay. Is that a worm?

No, that's a piece of rope. Don't eat that, otherwise you won't be able to shit for days.

All right. You're fucking smart.

I know.

I want to believe in BMISS. How do I do that?

Just pray and the answers will come.

Pray to whom?

To BMISS, of course.

Of course. They don't call you genius for nothing.

Maybe God looked like Leonardo? My phone rang: the comforting sound of someone remembering me. I hoped madly it was Chiara. She was giving me the cold shoulder again. More like freezing-zero-Kelvin shoulder. After our drinks and a great evening (her words, not mine), she disappeared again. Maybe she had crawled back into the giant vulva above her head.

There was no number.

Hello?

Krantik, it's me, Vineet. That was Pooja's brother. Star debater, president of the students' union in his college days.

Hi, Vineet. Thank god you called. How are you? How is she doing?

We trusted you, Krantik. We trusted you.

I know. I'm sorry.

You know we could have got anyone. There were offers from New York, London, investment bankers, McKinsey. And we chose you.

Yes. Yes, I know. Thank you.

And this is how you repay us?

No, you don't understand. I had nothing to do with it.

You were with her. In Amsterdam. Is that how you behave with your fiancée? We're a good family, I don't need to tell you that.

We didn't do anything. I mean . . . we just wanted to meet. I thought she would tell you about our meeting. I didn't do anything.

My dad can't even go back to his constituency. Yes, Pooja's dad was a member of parliament. Which is a huge deal. And yes, she could have married anyone. But my mom pursued her like she haggles for fish. Don't blame my mom, I don't. She thought, with my father dead and all, it would be good to marry into an influential family. God bless her soul. Like I said, around her, I'm like the Dalai Lama. In fact, I'm like the Dalai Lama on weed.

And our mother, Vineet continued, she's getting her palpitations again.

I'm so sorry. I hope she's okay. Where's Pooja? I lit a cigarette. On the road, the homeless man from our neighborhood peered into car windows hopefully. He had a beard like the ZZ Tops. And a giant hat, like Slash when he was riding his guitar in that deserted churchyard.

We've sent Pooja to our guru's retreat for some time out.

Great, I thought, first she tries to kill herself. And now she's being molested by some god-man. ZZ stretched his arm toward me. I nodded him off. He showed me the finger. So I slipped him a coin; I respond promptly to insult. Then he laughed, in a brotherly way. I walked away quicker.

You need to tell us, Krantik, what happened?

I've told you everything. We were talking, I had gone in to pay the bill . . .

Did you stay in the same room?

It's not like that. We had separate beds.

Guru-ji says if she has to recover, first she has to admit her sins. But she's not saying anything. There are dark planets on her path now. Maybe even your planets interfering with her life.

But you saw my horoscope! My Saturn phase is over.

We trusted your mother. But look at you.

Vineet, I'm sorry. I didn't do anything.

Why did you choose Amsterdam?

I didn't; she said she always wanted to go there.

But her flight was bought with your credit card, wasn't it?

That was a gift. I mean, you want me to look after her.

Did you do any drugs?

Vineet, I'm a manager. You know me: would an IIT graduate do something like that?

Don't give me that IIT bullshit. I can employ twenty IIT grads in my firm. Did you buy any drugs?

I don't even smoke. I just wanted to make her happy. That's all.

Krantik, you're a good kid. I know you. I can read people when I meet them. And you have a good heart. But you need to take responsibility now. Intention is not everything. Action is what matters. Do you understand?

Yes. Action is what matters.

We'll work with her. We'll make this work. I'm her brother, I'm always there for her. And you too. We're all in this together.

Of course. Of course.

I'll keep you posted. Guru-ji said it would take another six months. But when she's better, we'll go ahead with the wedding functions. Of course, when you're free. I'll let you know the date well in advance so you can plan your leave.

Okay. I had reached the bar. There were glowing lights, all melting into each other.

You understand what I'm saying?

Yes, I do. I fumbled for my cigarettes, pulled another one out.

You have a bright future, Vineet said. But if you fuck with us, he growled. Listen. If you fuck with us.

I tried to put the cigarette back. I missed.

Then you're fucking with the wrong family. We don't just take intentions. We take action.

Vineet . . .

You're like my brother. You know that? You're like my little brother.

Yes, I know.

Good night. You be good. Take care of yourself.

I will. Thank you, thank you.

The thing is MPs have shitloads of money. That's what my mom figured too, Mother Teresa that she is. (And no, I'm not talking about her all the time because of some Oedipal complex. I'm talking about her because she got me in this bloody mess.) And people with money, like Vineet's dad, can buy things. Like villas and spa packages and organic broccoli. A lot of money can buy crazy stuff: like goons with massive muscles and little patience. Or guns for hire. Surplus capital from Wall Street and from Indian MPs could also possibly end malnutrition and poverty. But I don't think Vineet would consider that a sensible use of his dad's resources. His game is more like guns for hire. Or renting daily brutalization in a prison for the target of his wrath (falsely accused and imprisoned of course, through a judicious use of said mammoth resources). Or targeting my mother. No, they couldn't. This was really taking my trip.

I tried Chiara's number again. This time she disconnected after two rings. Usually she just lets it ring. At least she's taking some action. Matters more than intention.

Ciao. Are you coming in or not? It was Federico. He grabbed me and did the man-cheek-kiss thing. One-two and now we're friends. I could still feel my aching jaw, little chips had broken out of a tooth. But I hated going to the dentist. And the tooth itself seemed okay now. Damaged, but hanging on. Like all of us.

Fede was sitting with an older woman. She was wearing something expensive: the kind of stuff where you don't need to show the brand. I was feeling sick, but now I had to stay.

That's Laura.

Ciao, I am Krantik. Federico's friend.

I know. He told me. She had pearls and a smile that gave nothing away.

What do you do?

Results-based management. Measuring the performance of different wings of our company . . .

I know what results-based management means. I run my own logistics company. My husband owns it, but I run it. Like most other things in his life. Except his cheap whores.

Hey, but I'm not a cheap whore. Or am I? Fede asked.

You're an indulgence, Fede, she said. You remind me of Haight-Ashbury.

You were in California in the sixties? I asked.

Do I look that old to you?

No, I meant maybe as a kid.

And Fede, you're not my pimp. You don't have to bring other exotic creatures to my table. He's not even that good-looking.

Hey, I'm not here for . . . what the . . . Fede was laughing, a low gurgle, I don't know if he was actually laughing or he thought it would sound good. A low gurgle, like a bong in motion.

I need to go.

Stay. Fede held my arm. I love you man, don't leave me with her. She may become my wife.

My life was filling up with crazy old men. And a girl I couldn't understand. It was like being in a Woody Allen movie.

He told me you didn't jump, Laura said.

What?

When he did his suicide run, you didn't jump from the car.

It was moving fast.

I would have slowed down. You didn't even freak out, Fede said. Pooja was at her guru's place: maybe they were doing laughter therapy. Or Vipassana meditation. Maybe she was levitating right now. And Chiara was probably at home, laughing at my missed calls, sprawled below a giant medieval vagina while her own was being plumbed.

I should be going, I have to finish some work. And I only came because Fede asked.

Listen, Kantip, Laura said.

Krantik, I said, there's an R and another K at the end.

Kran-tik. I'm sorry, I'm twenty years older than you. I'm sorry. Don't you Indians respect your elders?

Where did you hear that?

What?

About us Indians?

When I was in Goa.

I never heard that in Goa.

But you know football, right?

Yes, I do.

So who do you think's going to win?

If I cared enough, I would invest some thought into that question.

We always bet on Roma, Laura said.

What do you bet?

Stupid stuff. Like my marriage.

I have five euros.

If that's all you have that counts, you can put it in.

Do you guys know the players and their form well enough
to bet?

Does it matter?

I thought it would. I mean to enjoy the game.

Enjoy the game, said Fede. What? Are you a Coke com-
mercial now?

No, I was a status update, a photo waiting to be done up.
I was a story attached to an ass full of haemorrhoids. The
bar was filling up. Beers being lifted to waiting lips, glasses
filled with rotting grapes, smoke clouding into lungs on
the benches outside and spiraling out into a slowly wasting
world. There's an ozone hole bigger than our dreams and
it's letting the sun in. But Al Gore has a Nobel now. A Bangladeshi immigrant is doing a mime show outside the door.
He taps on a bald head here, pinches a moustache there.
People laugh, some dig into their pockets for the right kind
of change.

What happened there? I asked.

Roma just won a corner.

And that's good, right? You are betting on them.

That's great. It's the best thing that could happen.

What do you mean you're betting your marriage?

If Roma wins, then I'm filing for divorce.

No one knows the exact physics of football. Sometimes the ball swings because of the humidity in the air, sometimes the bounce is uneven if the football pitch is too dry, or changes direction if the grass on the pitch is too moist. Unless you're a twenty-foot computer processor from the 1970s, you can never know for sure where the ball will be. Or where your feet should be when you meet the ball in midair, midpitch. When you score a goal, you never know why it happened.

And if Roma loses?

If Roma loses, I do nothing. You can only bet on one result.

What about you? I asked Fede.

If Roma wins, then I'll sell my taxi.

And do what?

And mooch off Laura's alimony.

Who taught you this betting game?

Batukhan.

Who's Batukhan?

He taught us to watch football, said Laura.

Or to play our lives with football.

Do you want another beer?

I didn't know what I was doing there. Like a turtle on a terrace. But Turtle 8 often doesn't know why he does stuff. When everyone finishes his or her rotten-tomato supper, Turtle 8 has to walk to the eastern end of the terrace with Turtle 9, check the scene, and report back.

Turtle 8 to Turtle 9: Why're we doing this again?

To check on what's happening.

But nothing ever happens.

This is your job. So you better do it well.

What's a job?

It's what we have to do. If we do it well, everything will be okay.

Fine. (He continues walking, though his shell feels really heavy right now.) What will be okay?

You know, BMISS will look after us. Our unions will go well.

What's my union?

You and Turtle 4.

Oh, yes. That's important.

You guys are nice together. Why did you choose her?

I don't know. But this one time, a great leaf of lettuce was floating on her back. I could already smell the fungus. So I climbed on top of her.

Oh, my BMISS. That's so romantic. Okay, stop now. I'm getting teary-eyed, we need to pay attention.

And what if I want to go to the other end of the terrace.

You can't.

Why not?

That is the Corner of Chaos. Down that path lies the End of the MIHI World.

Okay. Then I guess I won't.

Hey, what's that? Hold back; it could be an intruder.

I think that's the same piece of rope.

You're getting smarter every day. I'm so proud of you, man.

Could this end in a draw? Laura asked. I had a new beer.

Yes. But not in this tournament, Fede said. They'll have a sudden death if the teams end up even.

Good. Just wanted to make sure. One can never be too prepared.

That's true. That's always true.

The stadium erupted. Roma scored. It was Fiorenzi. A bicycle kick, with the goal behind him, his body three feet above the ground and his feet above him. He was like a sculpture made of air.

VAN DAMME

I was on the metro on my way to the office. Again. Pressed against a nun, breathing down on her Christian-hijab head. She looked up, her eyes burning with piety, so much of it that her eyebrows had disappeared. No, that was only because she was Filipino. (What? Is that racist? No, it's not. There's nothing great about having well-toned eyebrows. Ask the Indian or Arab men who always have bushy eyebrows.)

Scendi? Are you getting off? she asked me. She's probably named after a saint. As a kid, she'd watch her father go out to sea, wait till he came back with lobsters, pincers tied but stupid eyes always open. You made it back? Yes, Saint Michael was kind. Who's Saint Michael? Protector of the seas. Then why doesn't he give you more fish? Because there's only one man who could multiply fish. Who's that: Felix who works at the factory? No, Jesus Christ. She didn't get it, so she went to pick up shells and kill those worms that burrow into the sand with Pedro, who told her he had a worm in his pants as well. And now when she remembers that morning, she crosses herself and does the Hail Mary twenty times.

No, I said. I stepped aside, while she got off.

There were also a couple of Bangladeshi immigrants in the
cabin. Okay, I lied earlier. I've spoken to them a few times.
Tough life they have here: eat potato and rice every day
(send every penny they can save back home to parents with
backaches and crutches, or to the Mafia immigrant smug-
gler who got them to Europe—he'll kill their mom and dad
and even their pet dog if he doesn't get his payments on
time). The Bangladeshis who sell umbrellas on the streets
of Rome wait for the first sign of rain to race out into the
streets. Living fifteen to a room, so if anyone needs to fuck,
they have to take the girl into the bathroom. It's true, these
things happen. The guys in the metro looked tired. They
were probably up all night working. Or in the loo.

Some people got off at Piramide, but we were still packed
with all our faces inches apart. The mornings are okay. You
can smell cologne. The evening rides are pickled in sweat
and semi-wiped asses. But sometimes in the evenings, you
see a woman with lost eyes, wondering why she's going back
to the same man. He wouldn't take out the washing and he
doesn't even pay the restaurant bill (once a month, when
they can afford to go out). It's the crisis, and yes, he's looking for a better job and he's always faithful, and he does
the dishes. But why the fuck is his underwear still out on
her side of the bed? She's had a long day at the office, and
her deserted eyes are seeing all the worlds she could have
inhabited, but that are now filled with prettier, richer people.
Maybe if she said yes to coffee with Mario who works in
accounts and then they made out in the bathroom near the
conference room, life would be okay. I often sit next to the

tumbleweed ladies. Sometimes all you feel is desolation. But sometimes, they want to claw their way out of their holes. And they'll do whatever it takes to feel the sun on the back of their necks again. And then I can smell woman. Which is even better than Chanel.

No, I don't look at just the women. That would be weird. I see men doing it all the time: even the cops in Rome, who stand around the piazzas pretending they're keeping guard (from what?) and all they do is the slow head turn with every pert ass that walks across the square. I never do that. Why can't people be more discreet?

There were these two guys, college kids, shiny jackets, swirling letters in red and white on their chests. They had friendship threads (or cancer bands?) on their wrists. The shorter one was saying something, and his friend was laughing hysterically, hands on the railing above him and face bent down and all crumpled up. *Basta basta*, he pleaded. Stop, stop. I couldn't understand a word of the joke. So I asked the joker the time. Just so he'd stop.

The crowd started thinning, and by the time the train reached my station (the last), I was sitting alone on a row of seats. In the middle, long-jacketed, back firm, hands on knees. If I had a long sword across my lap, I could have been a samurai. Ready for battle. Or for suicide.

Then I started walking. Office is like a numbing of the senses, seeping into you in slow, unyielding doses, like an insulin drip. Retirement by routine. Extinction through ennui. Maybe I should be a freelancer. Federico's office is his taxi. He told me he once had an office and a house (in California). It was a bad time, his last two years in the States after he was laid off: he couldn't get over his anxiety without medication, couldn't get medication without insurance, couldn't get insurance without a job, couldn't leave the house to look for a new job because of the anxiety. How did you fix that? Fixed itself, he said: lost house, lost savings, came back to Rome.

I walked through large sensor glass doors. Sometimes I take a step forward and then one step back, so the doors stutter open and closed. I like confusing technology. Scoring one for humanity. When I got into the elevator, because it was Monday, everyone was talking about the weekend. How was your weekend? What did you get up to? Went for a jazz concert in Villa Pamphili. I smiled at that. We had some great steak: this new place called Eataly. I smiled at that too. How do you spend a lifetime with people who are barely tolerable? How did the Buddha spend his weekend? Berries, some leaves, sun-dried, walk in the forest. Talked to some deer. Crazy times.

Markus wanted to see me. I didn't have the final draft of his project report ready.

Krantik, did you have a fabulous weekend?

Yes, I did. Markus goes to Bikram Yoga on Tuesdays and Thursdays.

Great, I love it when I see people filled with energy.

Yes, of course. Markus has tennis lessons on Mondays and Fridays, the coach made it to an ATP Tournament. Once. In 1984.

You need to channel that energy. You have some great ideas, I can see that. But it's all over the place.

I've been trying, Markus.

You know we have LBLF coming up? That's Looking Back, Leaping Forward, our annual employee evaluation exercise. They give the winners little mementoes: steel pyramids with the company logo embossed. I saw a dildo shaped like a pyramid once (in a video, not in real life).

Yes, I've filled out my form.

And I need to fill out your form too, in two weeks. I'll definitely say he's intelligent. I'll say he has good academic credentials. But, and I will have to say this, Krantik, there's a distinct lack of focus. He has not, repeat has not, delivered on his key assignments. And I'm sorry, if this report isn't ready on time, I'll have to say that.

Yes, I understand. Markus has four steel dildos on his table.

I need you to work on this, Krantik. You can check the industry network resource base, find the figures for a sector-wide reference, check our rate of return, talk to Claudio about the last financial analysis. Are you taking notes?

Yes, I am. My pen moved on paper.

Our board wants a company that's becoming more efficient. And I know it is. Why can't you show that?

I need to go over all the numbers.

Do a review of all customer interface indicators, say our current product base is being rolled out with maximum efficiency. We need to show a 3 percent improvement from the last report. Also say the next generation products are already in line with expectations. Use the phrase 'next generation.' Between his Bikram Yoga and his tennis, Markus straightens his back by sitting on his steel dildos. All four of them.

This is not just about our annual report, he continued. It's about your LBLF. Don't make yourself redundant. Not when you can be a star. You can be on this chair in ten years; you need to start planning now.

Of course. Markus has thirty-two straight teeth and he displays them for my viewing pleasure now. His lips are stretched back, and he's trying very hard to look like a father figure. Or a pyramid lover.

You are the future. YOU! His finger's up till I turn and leave. He can be dramatic sometimes; maybe he did theatre in college? He's drunk the Kool-Aid; in fact he's got a whole enema with it. But I don't hate him. I can be very Amish with people.

I met Massimo for a cigarette. We were standing in the sun, behind our office building and enclosed by large iron bars that ran across the backyard. This is not a metaphor; there was actually a row of ten-foot bars, each separated by a little gap. You could never make it out of there.

So you're working on the efficiency report?

How do you know that?

Everyone knows. Vito told me in the loo.

Why the hell is Vito talking about me? Vito was the guy everyone had a crush on. And he was blabbering nonsense all the time. This wasn't nonsense of course, I was working on the report. But it's none of his business. All the cute guys can get by without any intelligence or personality. Thankfully, I'm pretty hideous. (At least, compared to Brad Pitt or Ryan Gosling. Not compared to you sitting on your couch, or you in the gym pretending to work out to Fatboy Slim. I could be hotter than you.) The world doesn't take great notice of me. I need to survive on instinct honed through careful observation. So I have a very evolved understanding of the world.

Markus told him in the café.

Fuck.

People are worried. If your report's not good enough and if it doesn't tell the right story, the board's going to do some slash-and-burn around here. And if people lose their jobs, they'll probably blame you.

Great. Thanks for turning an insignificant report into the end of the world.

Maybe it is the end of the world.

No, it's not. There would be signs if it was the end.

What kinds of signs?

I think Oprah would stop talking.

And Van Damme would be involved in some way, he added.

Definitely Van Damme. Maybe a killing cyborg that also gives the perfect blow jobs. That would do away with straight sex and reproduction altogether.

What about the homophobes?

They could always become priests. I lit another cigarette, cherry to cherry. I wanted to be outside those iron bars. I didn't know where. I wanted to be an animal that didn't give a fuck. Maybe a llama. Nothing could bother a llama. Hey, Pedro's throwing a massive salsa party! Fuck that, I'm chewing my grass. Hey, your mother's being dragged away to the llama-Mac grinding factory. Can't you see, I'm sitting on this rock? Holy shit, you're being eaten alive by Van Damme and a meteor is hurtling down to kill all life on earth. I'll think about it when I'm done sniffing this tree.

If you could be anywhere, where would you be? Massimo asked me. Sometimes he can read my thoughts. I often think of his father sitting at home getting high on the marijuana tree.

I'd be anywhere but here.

That's not true, there are worse places to be.

Such as?

You could be a miner in South Africa, getting your lungs lined with copper and your eyes filled with mercury.

Or I could be chained to a wall in someone's sex cellar.

Or I might be in Google, Massimo said. No one ever leaves the building. And they pretend it's some kind of twenty-four-hour fun-day, get your pet over, grab a Coke from the fridge, get dinner in the office, hang out with all the other cool Googlers so you don't even need a social life outside. Congratulations: this is the life you've always dreamed of. He twisted his dead butt into the ashtray.

Sounds horrible. How do you know so much about the work there?

I keep applying. And never hearing back. Massimo goes to visit his dad every weekend. And now, he's trying to sniff something on his nails. I hope his nails weren't investigating down his ass when I wasn't looking. I've seen that happen.

Are you okay? After your trip back home. Everything okay?

Yes, of course. And then I added: Only my ass is bleeding.

That happens to me all the time. Too much meat.

Liesbeth mailed and asked if Massimo and I wanted to hang out. I said I had too much to do, buried under work, will need all evening to plough through. Then Massimo called on my extension and said I should come: she might even bring Sandra along. But I told him I couldn't. And that Markus was calling me, so I had to hang up.

I stopped at the supermarket and picked up some aubergine, zucchini, and minced beef. And then some random shit: one of the only two Pringles flavors available and Diet Coke. When I got home, I sliced the veggies really thin; it's nice to have them mushy with the beef. While the meal was cooking (I like it to simmer for a long time), I sat on the laptop and before I knew it, there were five Facebook tabs open, three Cracked articles, and half a dozen reddit pages. Liesbeth had gone to Madagascar and had pictures of golden beaches and turquoise skies, also a fisherman who held a crab by a rope. Pooja's wall was inactive, but someone had tagged her in old school pictures. She was in the second row in pigtails and her male classmates were commenting on how they all had a crush on their class teacher who was sitting in the front row centre, her sari falling perfectly into place. On reddit, I saw a skinned thumb; the bone sticking out after a home-décor accident, but thankfully the poster still had his iPhone with him in the operation room so he could post the picture. Someone's dog had killed and dragged home a giant mole and it was now on the living room carpet, its shoulder torn into shreds and its mouth still wide open in shock. At a party, a fat guy with only a party cap on and a star tattooed on his bicep was trying to set his dick on fire. He also had a brown scarf on, but he didn't think that worthy of destruction. I opened a few office files, but obviously I didn't work on them. Switched between them a few times. Wrote an e-mail to Chiara and then discarded it. Wrote another one, saved it in my drafts.

The beef smelled good now. I had added turmeric, coriander powder, and cumin. I waited at the window for some time, I could see a bar downstairs, people trickling out to smoke, ask each other for lighters, and sip their cocktails in the pauses between conversations. One guy leaned over and kissed his girlfriend. She tugged his scarf; it wasn't cold enough for a scarf, but he looked good with it. Above them, street lamps were strung on wires that stretched across the road. On one end of the road rose the remnants of an ancient Roman temple, about five storeys high. It must have been massive. Where I was standing on the second floor must have been inside the temple.

When I finished eating, I had some music on, but I wasn't sure what was playing. I lay down on the couch and stared at the ceiling. There were all these voices in my head. Maybe not different voices, just one voice saying lots of different things. But I asked them to stop anyway.

MORNING

I got my nightmares from Netflix and my poetry from Facebook. The poetry wasn't great, but the nightmares weren't that bad either.

I had been watching a true crime series. I saw a chain saw whining through a woman's limbs, its sound shredding the air into purple, the hand of the murderer shaking while pressing down, jagged bones with ribbons of meat hanging off them like confetti strewn around a basement floor. I couldn't see the monster that did this. But I was deep in the series. I wasn't the murderer, but I was mute.

I dreamed that I walked into the largest shopping complex in a riverside town that used to be a village and bought a nightmare. They had discounts and blockbuster offers. They said they had the latest models and I would keep coming back for more. Back home, I unwrapped the packaging and found a gun and a bullet and a question. The question floated up in the air and then coiled around my head. I wanted to imagine it was a crown of thorns or a halo. But I found a mirror and saw that it was a dunce cap.

There was an open window next to where I sat in the morning. I could have flown out and seen the world. I could also have jumped out and seen no more. The world was out there, and so was the end of the world.

I went to Ikea and bought myself some plastic furniture.

Come ON Take a TRIP

The end of that week, Friday, Liesbeth called me. I was checking for a gastroenterologist to get my ass examined. Again. She does have a heart of gold, Liesbeth. It's soft and malleable, also it deforms under stress: Tanzanian malnutrition gets her down, so does Wall Street arrogance. And repeated refusals. So I said I was coming. Sometimes she beats her heart into a pulp and smears it in thin paste over ugly things, to make little gold trinkets. I may bitch about her, but we end up hanging out a lot. And she had some good stuff, she said.

I got on the metro and found a seat at once, which is always a miracle. There was a blonde girl opposite me with glasses on. I looked at her and she was looking at me, and then we both turned away. An older man was standing near me. I didn't offer him my seat; he had a beard like Sean Connery so probably didn't need it.

The metro had cradled us down one stop when a hobo entered the carriage. He had no shoes, and no pants on. Just a long coat that went down to his knees and a dirty cap. He bared his ugly misshapen teeth. And then he slouched against a railing and started his speech. I couldn't understand some of it, but this is more or less what he said (in Italian of course; because I know you don't read Italian, I've written it out in English): Good evening, ladies and gentlemen, I'm a poor man, poorer than any of you. I don't have enough money for a meal and haven't eaten a full meal in days. So if you have some spare change, you can give it to me.

He stank up the whole compartment; he hadn't showered since the Berlin Wall fell. (Of course, we don't remember that, do we? No one remembers the wall being torn down, at least not since the two towers fell.) And it was as if he just read out his litany, there was no feeling. He didn't need any pleading: he was probably thinking, I don't need shoes, hell I don't even need pants, do you think I need your money. He had no drama. And he had no dignity. We like our poor dignified.

So I took out a few coins. I had to reach over and drop them in his hand, which didn't stretch far; it was probably fossilized with dirt.

Everyone looked away. Fuck you all, I thought. Fuck you and your purses and your iPads, fuck your hair and your shoes, fuck your mom who died of cancer and your brother who's just been diagnosed, fuck your red skintight pants, fuck you if you didn't get your promotion, and fuck you if you lost your job. Fuck you if you're dying and fuck your newborn child too. I'm getting out of here. It was my stop anyway.

I was calmer as I climbed into the skies on the escalator. Sometimes my anger is fake. Often my sorrow is fake too. If I don't fill my soul with wind and bluster, the world may know it's empty and crush it like a Coke can. You could add gold plating on it, but it's still just an empty Coke can.

When I was walking to Liesbeth's place, I crossed a yard with books, furniture, CDs, a birdcage, some old suits littered on the lawn. So I walked in. It was an estate sale: some guy had kicked the bucket and now his whole life was for sale. Everything he owned at least. "Todd Williams, lover of books, birds, and beauty in the world. Husband, father, friend. We will miss you." The placard read. An American; I wasn't surprised. No Italian family would sell their memories; this whole place is built on memories. People milled around the tables, picking up stuff, putting them down respectfully, as if the lampshade was dying of kidney failure too. I went through the books; I read a lot, but you've probably figured that out by now (and no, not just random websites, sometimes actual books too). Dostoevsky for three euros, but he was too heavy; Safran Foer for five euros, nice but I've got most of them; maybe Jeanette Winterson since I haven't read anything but *Oranges*. And then I saw the Graham Greene. He had only one. *The Quiet American*. Funny that was on sale here. Because the only quiet American is a dead American.

When I reached Liesbeth's place, she asked me if I had paper. I said no.

But I told you I had stuff.

So I assumed you had paper. In fact, I even brought the rolling machine.

What do we roll with? Toilet paper?

We could do that, Massimo said, and then smoke that shit.

I can do it in a cigarette, I offered. I started twisting the tobacco out of my cigarette while Liesbeth scooped a little to mix with her weed.

On my way here, I saw a yard sale. Some guy who died and now all his belongings are up for sale. It's in one of those big houses in Garbatella.

I've never seen that here.

No, he's American. Was American.

What do they have?

Everything: his walking stick, his books, bedside table, his hats including the slightly worn ones.

That's terrible, Liesbeth said, it's like they're getting rid of him entirely.

No. I think it makes perfect sense, I said. He's dead, what's the point in hanging on to his used underwear?

In Japan, they sell used underwear, Massimo said.

To who?

They have vending machines for used ladies' underwear. Men queue to pick them up. Probably take them home for some conversation.

If I had a lover who died, Liesbeth said, I would never sell his stuff.

If I died, I would ask whoever's left behind to sell it all, I said. In fact, I'd ask them to sell all my memories too. Sell my first date, my first time on a plane, the first day in an office.

I'd sell all my days in the office, Massimo said.

For how much?

Anyone can have them for free.

So we made a list of memories that people could sell.

First pet: You pay 400 euros.

Naming the first pet: 5,000 euros (because you also get a lifetime of passwords)

First-time sex: 30 euros (it's never divine, it's always a mess, and you'd rather start with the pro-category anyway)

Marriage: Pay what you want

First kiss: 3,000 euros, if teenage fumbling in a corner and magical. 40 euros if adult and desperate.

My holiday in Palolem where I was with the girl and I had the greatest sandwich in the world: I would never sell that.

I was still dropping tobacco out of the cigarettes. Drop, drop the tobacco. Sprinkle some on the weed. Then drop the cigarette on the table. It will come alive again, filled with magic.

Drop, drop through the water, float inside. But then you find you're sinking.

We moved to the balcony to smoke. There was a deserted hospital in front of us, Liesbeth claimed she heard sounds from the building every Thursday. And there's a huge palm tree. We could be in the Middle East. Only then the buildings would be crumbling with explosions, not slow motion for centuries, like in those start-stop videos. Massimo is trying to inhale as deep as he can. And while he waits with his lungs full, he twists his fingers into a Hindu-lotus-cow position. He's such a jerk. I took the joint from him. Nothing was happening. Below us, a man muttered to himself on the streets. And then he held up his empty hand to his ears and started screaming. *Porca miseria, porca miseria.* Into his invisible phone. Fuck misery. In Rome, the object of fuck

works along a well-defined gradation. You start with fuck
the snowman. And then fuck misery. And then you work
your way up. Till you reach Madonna (the original virgin,
not the 1980s rocket-bra Madonna).

Who's he shouting to?

Whoever's on the other end. Rome is filled with crazy
people. I mean, literally crazy people. They had an asylum
on the outskirts of town, and then they had to shut it down,
fiscal tightening etcetera (I like writing etcetera, it's so much
classier than the abbreviation). And since no one came to
pick up the inmates, they let them loose on the streets.
Which is probably nicer than being locked up. We're all on
the streets. Actually, most of us are locked up in offices to
keep the roads safe.

We smoked three joints in a row. Massimo and Liesbeth
had gin and tonics. I had an orange juice. When we walked
back to her living room, it happened. I was unstuck from
time. The room was floating, and so was I.

Where did you get this stuff?

From this guy at work.

Does he have a name?

Gordon. He knows a great dealer. Says this is grown in labs
in the north.

This is brilliant.

By unspoken agreement, I twisted another cigarette open and Liesbeth started cleaning another bud. Heart of gold she had, probably deposited on earth by some meteorite, like most of the earth's reserves. A woman who rolls, who knows a great dealer. Once we danced and got a little close, but that was it.

Are you looking at my boobs?

No, I'm not.

I think you were, Massimo said. You weren't even blinking, you were so overwhelmed by their magnificence.

I was thinking. It was the gazing into the middle-distance look, and your boobs just happened to be there.

If you were, you can admit it. We're all family here, Massimo said. I'm often overwhelmed by their magnificence.

Their magnificence! Really? Liesbeth asked.

Of course.

So, you guys aren't just here for the free weed?

No. We're here to worship you.

If only either one of you were any better looking.

Thanks, I said. Great time to remind us of our inadequacies. When we're stoned and paranoid.

I'm joking. She finished mixing. I went to the loo. As soon as I started pissing, I remembered what I had had for lunch. Asparagus. I was zooming out asparagus piss. Have you ever smelled it? It filled up the whole bathroom. This really powerful smell. But on the edges, you can also feel its life-affirming quality: something so powerful can only come from a good vegetable.

You know about poppers? Liesbeth asked me when I got back.

Poppers?

Gay men use it a lot.

Never heard of them.

When they're making out, they pop a couple.

What does it do?

I don't know. But it's supposed to be great for sex.

Maybe it loosens the anal muscles, I said. Liesbeth laughed. She looked nice laughing. Pretty. Chiara looked great laughing; Chiara wasn't pretty. I mean not pretty-pretty. Her hair frizzed all around her face, clearly under no control or with no design. I was thinking of Chiara again. I made sure I looked away, towards the TV, this time.

That's when Sandra walked in. She kissed Massimo and Liesbeth hello and then me. And then she held my hand.

You can talk to us, she said.

I am talking.

No, you can tell us if you need anything. I didn't say anything. My hand was still in hers. I tried looking melancholy. I wished I wore glasses. When I should feel sad but I don't, I think of other people. You're an executive on the ninety-fifth floor, with your brand new spotted tie, surveying the city that you will control someday. And then you see a plane flying, too close to the ground and then too close to you. Too soon, it always comes too soon.

You're buying naan because your cousin Muzammil has brought some great mutton curry from the old man near the chowk. You're in Nadeem's bakery where you always buy your bread, because he never cheats you and once he even gave you some of his hashish. He's always clucking when you talk about Muzammil: used to be such a quiet kid, till he picked up the gun and the Quran. You don't have time for Nadeem's lecture because the roganjosh is waiting at home. And then you hear a whistling in the air. It's coming from far away. Nadeem leans out of the window, and you know from the shock in his eyes that it's too late. You knew when the troubles started that one day you would be stuck in a place where it was too late.

My hand was still in Sandra's. Liesbeth had put on the Grateful Dead and I wanted to hum along or move my head to the beat, but I couldn't. It's difficult to hum along to them. I don't even like their music, I think they're like an overrated country-folksy-boy-band with too much hair on their faces. (What? You can insult my god and I can't insult yours?) My hand was frozen and I couldn't stand near the table like a statesman all night. So I sat down and Sandra rubbed my shoulders. I poured a little vodka for myself, but it was suddenly really heavy. So when Massimo switched the music to RATM, I stood up and said we should move before we get too lazy. Rage is always a good trip.

We took a taxi. Outside, young men ran with the dogs and the women balanced their stilettos on the cobblestones. I had gone to a village in Umbria with Pooja (when she came to visit me in Rome) and we saw groups of old men and women sit on separate benches like in a high-school social event. They laughed at the same jokes they had heard from the same people for fifty years. Their faces were ridged like the valleys of Tuscany. Pooja was taking photographs while I sat on a parapet and watched the people. Later I asked her what she clicked and she said she was checking out the barks of trees. I thought that was an intimate moment. But then she had an album up on Facebook: Talking to Trees. I wasn't in the album, only the trees.

Sandra was laughing. Liesbeth had told her about the poppers. Sandra asked if she had any, but none of us really knew what they were.

We reached the club, which was a warehouse that had been taken over. In Rome, communists and anarchists are always taking over old buildings and converting them into clubs. Which is what communism should be about. And then they abuse Berlusconi who's as fucked up as they come. Berlusconi's worse than a llama: he has no shame. He's also a fascist, but I never know what that means. And he loves hanging around with women young enough to be his granddaughters. For Berlusconi, God is probably a big blue Viagra pill in the sky.

The club was as random as they come. In one corner, the walls were on fire, I mean digitally with strobe lights and displays. People were jerking their arms and legs, all moving to some trance. In our corner, a long cloth rope hung from the ceiling: a man and a woman in tight leggings were twisting around in the sky. He split his legs open upside down while gripping the cloth with some part of his body, I couldn't even tell which. And she sat in a Buddhist pose on his upside-down crotch. I think the dance was trying to tell us something: have more sex, or get your hernia checked.

Then there was some music at our end, and I was floating again. In my own time, which is always nice. It was hip-hop dub-step something, but nice, not with a rabid beat. Then Sandra dragged us to a room outside the main hall. Hangers full of old jackets for sale, people sitting around unvarnished tables smoking joints and talking about Foucault. Some of her friends had set up a stall, where they were taking old Polaroid pictures of groups: they called it Re-View, Re-Act. We had to choose our props and soon I had shades with pizza slices on the brows and a bowler hat on me. I smiled and they clicked. Once. And then again because we switched around our props. Once more, *uno due tre.* I smiled again.

Smile click post share. Smile click post share. Repeat.

Which is your favourite item?

Where?

Among all these, Liesbeth asked. Everything on their stall was older than me.

It's like we're the items, and we're actually photographing the scarves and the hats.

You're not a scarf.

Why not? Because I have a soul? I asked.

No, Sandra said, because you couldn't be half as cool as that scarf.

I wouldn't mind being an accessory.

What kind of accessory?

I don't know.

I thought of a few. Only by the time I did, we were already out of the stall. Sandra and I were dancing. She was doing the ironic *Pulp Fiction* dance. I was doing a clueless pretending to be stoned while actually being stoned dance.

I could be a piece of bacon on Lady Gaga's ass. Or I could be a gun in MIA's hands. Or Elton John's shades.

Would you rather be Shah Rukh Khan's stutter or Clint Eastwood's half-shut eyes?

Would you rather be a pair of crazy eyes in a Kurosawa movie or Björk's bobbing head?

Would you rather have been the public toilet with George Michael inside or the car with Hugh Grant inside?

And then the music came racing into my head. They had turned up the volume. They had a live act on: I hadn't even seen the stage. The act featured these two raging gay men. One in a skintight pink leotard and the other in a long green dress.

ROME! Are you READY?? Green Dress shouted out. He knew we were all fucked out of our brains.

I CANNOT hear YOUU. The crowd roared. And then they turned up the bass.

Da-BOOMM-da-da-BOOM. The heavy beat skewered right through me and rattled me inside, kidney, liver, everything. All around me, people started shaking their heads slowly, and then faster. The bass blew away bits of my mind. The bits that I could never hold on to anyway.

Here, Sandra dropped something in my hand. Little beads, like lumps of gnarled skin, covered my palm.

What is it?

Magic mushroom.

If I smile for Polaroid photos, I suppose I can put stuff in my mouth too. So I downed it all. It was horridly bitter, so I chased it with the vodka in my hand.

Then I waited for it to kick in.

Hey ROME, are you HERRE??

Da-BOOM-da-da-BOOMM. It sounds crazy, but that was the beat.

Come ON Take a TRIP. Lady wore a gown but had a voice like James Hetfield.

Come ON Take a TRIP. A foot in front of me, Sandra swiveled her ass to the beat.

And then I was moving too.

Come ON Take a TRIP.

They are thinking about the sea. A voice blared inside my head. But no, it wasn't inside my head. It was a voice like asparagus piss: metallic, but crumbling around the edges into something going crazy.

It was Chiara.

I turned around. Who?

Your landlord's turtles, she was screaming into my ear. When they have sex, they're thinking about the sea.

Come ON Take a TRIP.

Why would they think about the sea?

Because that's where they come from.

NAMES

We danced for a bit. And then we stepped outside for a smoke. Chiara and me, of course. Everything was blazing lights around me, and sounds that melted into each other. We were at the dead end of a street; abandoned cars lined the walls, shimmering grey and rust. Maybe it was the mushroom. I heard strains of Marley.

How have you been? Chiara asked me.

Okay. Same shit, different day.

Are you always filled with one-liners? Like a Guy Ritchie movie?

They're spontaneous, I swear.

Maybe you have a list.

A list of what?

Of one-liners that you carry with you.

And I pluck out a line whenever I need to? Wouldn't that be more effort than just making them up?

But you would rather be funny than real. Have you met your landlord since we saw him?

Leonardo? Had a beer with him once. He took off his shirt.

Because he was trying to seduce you?

Because he said he wanted to feel free.

She pulled out a cigarette. I offered my lighter. And she steadied my hand as she lit up.

What do you do in your free time?

Is this a speed-dating question?

No, it's a 'I hope I'm not in a dark alley with a rabbit-molester' question.

No rabbits. Only squirrels.

Was that on your list of one-liners?

Whiffs of weed hung in the air around us. I could still hear the booming beat from inside. I could feel it in my ass. Probably the prostate, that's apparently where men get turned on the most. But maybe it wasn't the music playing with my prostate. It was Chiara. She was talking to some random guy, unruly hair, a torn sweater, calculatedly casual (all rugged, but actually all planned). They turned their hands in the air like Italians do, making pointy pyramids to make a point. Light was glowing off their bodies. Sometimes we are in a movie: everything moves so perfectly.

Hey, Krantik, I want you to meet someone. She pulled the guy's sweater. This is Marco.

Hi, I'm Krantik.

Hey, how're you doing?

Good, good. That's a nice band. I couldn't think of anything else to say.

They sure are, saw them last summer in Camden Town.

I didn't say anything.

London.

Yes, I know.

Of course. Only one shouldn't assume. You know, we stay long enough in a city and you think it's the centre of the world.

Rome is the centre of the world, I said.

No. It hasn't been for a thousand years. Chiara had her head bent up towards him while he spoke.

I was just being polite.

No need to be. He smiled. And I didn't want to admit it, but it was a smile coming from a big heart. But maybe it was a big plastic, cellophane teddy heart.

I'll leave you guys to talk. Chiara kissed him briefly and he went back inside. I sipped from my glass. There were two crescent slices of lemon floating in my drink. What the hell were they doing there?

Is that your boyfriend?

He's not my boyfriend.

Yes, I remember, you said sort of boyfriend.

He's my husband. She sucked at her cigarette, her claw clamped around the butt. Why the fuck did she need four fingers to hold a cigarette?

Great. You guys look perfect together. All you need is two blonde kids in your lap.

She sniggered. Yes, sniggered.

Don't be ridiculous, Krantik.

I'm not ridiculous. I know what I am.

What's that?

I'm your weekend mistake. The one that gives you a bad hangover. The drink that you didn't even finish. But the one that goes banging inside your skull the next day.

You're fucking stupid.

Did you pray and ask Mother Mary for forgiveness. For your mistake.

Why should I ask 'Mother Mary' about anything? What would she know about sex?

Listen, I know it's all okay. Everything is okay. I'm totally cool with whatever. But I don't want to be your regret for your lost youth or anything.

My lost youth?

You look thirty-plus to me. And that's not young anymore. Or, you know, I don't want to be some random guy you make out with because, I don't know, Marco didn't get you anything from Harrods or whatever.

Will you SHUT the FUCK up? Will you stop being an entitled pig, whining about your bruised ego?

I sipped more of my drink.

I like you, I really like you, she said.

Yes, I know. Now you'll do the condescending I like you, you're just not my type. And you know, Marco's the gentlest soul in the world; I couldn't do anything behind his back.

Hey, hey, stop talking. For like a minute.

Okay.

Nothing's happening behind Marco's back. Why should anything happen behind his back?

He knows?

Of course he knows. Why wouldn't he know? He's my closest friend.

And your husband.

But first, he's my closest friend.

Great. So, I'm ruining a perfect marriage. Now I'm a home-breaker.

You're not a home-breaker. Who even uses words like home-breaker?

I do, when I meet desperate housewives.

Fuck you. It's not like you think. We get along well together, you and me. Isn't that true?

Yes, I think so. Now I was sober. The mushroom's supposed to last five hours. And here I am, thirty minutes later, my feet turning into lead.

So if we like each other, we can meet.

Sure, for coffee. I'd love that. After all, we are such good friends and we go back such a long way, we could meet and talk about our university days, since we share such a deep platonic bond.

No, I mean, we can meet and we can talk. Or we could go for a movie. Or whatever. Eat pasta. And then if we want, we can fuck. Or kiss. Or we can look at each other naked and play Scrabble. Do whatever we want.

I took her drink and started sipping it. If she was taking my trip, I could at least steal her drink.

Okay, this is how it works. Are you calmer?

I'm listening.

Marco and I are not into the whole bourgeois marriage as a sacred institution scene. We meet other people when we want. You know, this whole love thing, I don't know how it became so insular and so fucking possessive.

I breathed in. Breathed out. I tried to not be there, but I was.

And you and I, we can be friends. You want another name? Lovers? That's not happening yet. Why do you need a name for it?

This is crazy. I took out a cigarette. I'm always doing that, when I don't know what else to do.

It's called an open relationship.

I know what it's called.

I thought you wanted a name for it.

LISTENING TO BOMBS

And how long have you had the pain?

Off and on. About three years.

Only when you pass stool?

When I'm shitting, yes. But sometimes it stays for two or three days.

More scribbling. He was paying attention; I like doctors who pay attention, who take their patients seriously.

How much pain when you pass stool?

On a scale of one to ten, if ten is unbearable pain, then I think six or seven at the time of shit . . . passing stool. During the day, about two or three.

A lot of pain. Fingers flying over what looks like Greek on the notepad.

Yes, six or seven on a scale of ten. You can write that.

I understand.

Of course, I don't know what ten is actually. Because I have never faced unbearable pain.

Okay, okay.

And then two or three during the rest of the day. He wasn't writing anymore.

And the blood, what colour is it?

On the toilet paper, it's bright red. In the water, it's light red: violet? Or pink.

Good, bright red is good. Does anyone in your family have haemorrhoids?

My cousin Vicky. He gets it when he drinks too much, he told me.

Can I examine your belly, could you lie down here please?

I lay down and looked up on his roller bed-sheet.

Pull up your shirt. And then he started pressing everywhere. Does this hurt?

A little.

And this?

A little.

What about here?

A little.

There is some stiffness.

I had seen the symptoms on the online forums. Alicia_47 from Ohio had difficulties for a few months before she went to the doctor and then it was too late. Big_heart_2002 had congested bowels, he spent months worrying it was colon cancer. He didn't die, but he had to get his intestines tied up in a loop to shit.

Is it bowel obstruction?

I don't know. We'll have to do a test.

What kind of test?

Have you ever had a colonoscopy done?

Not yet. I knew the drill: no soft drinks, tea, or coffee from the day before, no nuts, seeds, hulls, skins, no red, blue, purple colouring. After the medication to clear your bowels, stay close to a loo the whole day. Very close. Waseem_bigdk from Hyderabad had to attend office for an urgent client meeting. Didn't end well.

We need a clear bowel for a good test. Let me explain.

I listened. I already knew. What if in the future, gay parents became ultraconservative. And if one such set had a gay kid

but didn't want him doing anything before he got married.
No sex, definitely no poppers. Maybe they'd prescribe anti-
poppers, to freeze up the butt (like virginity belts or something). Anti-poppers blessed by the Pope.

Sometimes I shock myself with the vaguely disconcerting
territory my thoughts meander into. Not because they're
troubling. But because if I don't hold back, they may ven-
ture even further into the realm of the unspeakable. (Realm
of the unspeakable! That has a nice and medieval ring to
it.) But then if we're free to say anything online, why can't
we do that in our internal monologues. I think the Internet
is our collective monologue. Elon Musk thinks we're in the
Matrix. I think he's crazy. A voice just told me to say that.

The doc told me about the powder (orange flavor), the gel
(rub gently in circles), the procedure (happens all the time),
his expertise (if there's anything in there, I'll find it). What
can you find so deep inside a man? Where does our soul
reside? In the heart? Chinese meditation books talk about
the base of the spine. Don't some of those Hindu draw-
ings talk about the top of the head? Every time there's an
extraordinary new scientific discovery, I love how Indians
claim it for themselves. Higgs boson? Our Vedas spoke
about it 3,000 years ago when they mentioned that which
cannot be defined. NASA and Mars Challenger or Discovery? It's down to the Indians again: you see, Aryabhata discovered the zero. None of this would have been possible
without the zero.

When will you be free? What about Tuesday: three days
from now?

Doctor, how much will it hurt?

What do you mean?

The operation, on a scale of one to ten.

Probably zero. You will be under anesthesia.

Zero is Indian. But we don't really know what it means. Sometimes I feel like the square root of -1: totally imaginary, but with some apparent function. I didn't say these things.

Also, has anyone in your family had cancer?

I didn't know for sure. But I smiled: holding your cheeks firm helps you concentrate. Resist fear.

When I walked back home I was feeling better. It's just a test, and if there's anything, he'll find it. I could see the tumour inside my intestines: bulbous with little tentacles growing into different organs. Maybe the tumour had a name, Larry. I'm guessing. Larry doesn't know my name either.

I called Massimo and told him about the operation. He said shit. And then he said he could come over and meet me for a drink. I said no, thanks. Chiara had called once. For the first time, I didn't answer. I didn't know what to say. Maybe I should spend the rest of my life taking photographs of my food and uploading them on Instagram or

Facebook? Sometimes it feels like time is cooking us all the time, preparing us. Have you ever seen the Goya painting where the god (I think Saturn) is eating his children? Supposed to be about time and generations and the inevitable. We spend so much time meeting people we allegedly know, and they're talking about stuff: the latest movie; aborigines and their rights; Bikram Yoga and did you know the positions squeeze your internal organs; have you seen the Double Rainbow and what about the new Mitt Gangnam mash-up; so in Kurosawa's *Rashomon* what was the actual story; if the report doesn't display a significant growth in efficiency the board may have to take some drastic action, and I mean drastic; how was the weekend; does that even matter because so much of art criticism is about perspective that no single analysis could ever be true; what is the director thinking anyway how could we ever tell, and then Zizek said the first floor of the girl's apartment was her super-ego; crazy weekend; couldn't believe he would do something like that, they looked like the perfect couple. You listen and you nod. Then you say something more. Either you say the same thing, or you say something new. And then the new becomes old.

We are all being eaten alive.

I met a young man smoking a cigarette. He had a beard with curly wisps drooping down his face. I asked him where Piazza Venezia was. He wanted to know if I wanted the museum entrance or the entrance to Campidoglio, because I could walk to either side and it would take me the same time. I said I could do both. He probably did archaeology in college and could have told me about the Etruscans who built Rome. But then, why aren't they just called Romans? Because Rome was a city that had no people, only the hills and the water as clear as the spring skies (his words if he were talking to me, not mine). After Romulus and Remus had suckled on the wolf's teats, Romulus founded the city. Only the city had no people, so he offered asylum to any criminal or outlaw who wanted to join him (a lot of this riff-raff were the Etruscans). A bit like Australia, without the cricket team. Once upon a time, the archeologist thought he would spend a lifetime digging through the rubble in Ostia and discover, all by himself one late autumn night after fifteen years of investigation, whether the Trojan refugee Aeneas had truly founded Rome (instead of the popular wolf-twins myth which our friend never really believed). Even if only twenty people in the whole world truly appreciated the archeologist's work, he would be fulfilled because he had answered a 3,000-year-old question.

But now he works in marketing, and only uses his entire education for trivia when he sits for Easter lunch with his girlfriend's family. Her dad is a banker and nods every two minutes to the young geek's lectures. His opinion of his daughter's boyfriend approaches something like contempt. So he asks the boy to pass the olives.

I said thank you (I always say *grazie*, there is so much to be thankful about. Actually, not really.) and walked towards home. I crossed Via Galvani where Chiara lived. On one end of Via Galvani was the Protestant cemetery: just outside the city walls since non-Catholics weren't allowed to be buried inside the Holy City. Gramsci is decomposing there. So is John Keats. On his tombstone it says: Here lies one,

whose name was writ in water. But who could have written
that? Jesus?

And on the other end of Via Galvani is the modern art
museum. It used to be a slaughterhouse, still has the giant
hooks where they hung the cattle. Sometimes, they string
up paintings or photos on the hooks. Between marinating
cows and nameless poets, Chiara and her vagina stew on
the ground.

Where is Kurt Cobain buried? Did Eddie Vedder smoke
his ashes (rock stars don't do that kind of thing anymore)?
What should we do when Lady Gaga dies? Cover a turkey
with strips of her skin? And then Justin Bieber could have
the turkey for Thanksgiving. That could be the first sign
of the end of the world. We think too much about climate
change. We need to focus on the real issues: is a world possible after Lady Gaga and Oprah, another world where
Shah Rukh Khan isn't smirking and Amitabh isn't playing
pimped-up forty-year-olds on screen and Sachin Tendulkar
isn't adjusting his crotch while he takes guard? There is no
other world but this one.

In the evening, Federico called me again and asked if I
wanted to catch the next game. On my way to the bar, I
ran into Leonardo, he was geared up in his uniform. One
hand extended in support to the old lady who stays opposite his flat. She was ninety years old (claimed she was
107 and remembers the First World War). He called her
grandmother, Nonna. Every evening when Leonardo was
allegedly in town, he took her out. Nonna once had a son

named Marco. Marco died, so she's left with just Leonardo who doubles up as a son-neighbor figure. His turtles probably double up as her grandchildren.

Hey, Krantik. Where are you going?

Going to watch a game at Il Cazzo. Nonna nodded. Or her head was nodding; I don't think she controls her movements anymore.

Che cosa e Cazzo? she asked.

Cazzo is where you go to learn the meaning of life, Leonardo said to her. You don't worry about this, Nonna. Young people need their alcohol; they need to make sense of the world.

Nonna cackled and I could see her yellowed, toothless gums. Leonardo's always saying crazy shit to her. She's losing her mind with dementia/Alzheimer's. Thinks Leonardo's her son most of the time.

You remember Krantik, don't you? He asked her.

Si si. Ma tu non sei Italiano?

No, I said, sono Indiano.

Cazzo.

When I got to the bar, I saw Fede and Laura with another man.

Krantik, my man. Fede broke off to hug me. His lips were swollen and a whole patchwork of bruises ran across half his face.

What happened?

A small accident.

I'm sorry.

Don't be. It went off perfectly, he said.

There was a guy between them; he had a wizened face, like a dry mango, and a long coat that trailed on the ground.

That's Batukhan.

Hi, he drew out a hand; the other was still drumming the glass. He had a drooping moustache. He looked like an Eskimo or Central Asian, not swarthy South Asian or Middle Eastern. (What does a Middle Eastern person look like? I want to say sinister, but I suspect that's because I watch so much *24*, so I won't say it. But now I've already said it.) Looked like he had a long-barreled gun in his coat. Or a piece of dried yak meat.

Are you Hindu? He was fluent in English; even a hint of an English accent.

My parents are. Maybe I am.

Which is your favourite god?

Shiva.

Why Shiva? Isn't he a bad guy?

No, he hangs out with the badasses, demons etcetera (yes, I did that again). And smokes a lot of weed.

That's a good reason to like him.

The best I could think of.

Jesus is cannibalized every day, Laura said. Perfect for BDSM types.

You don't believe in Allah?

I don't know what he looks like.

Do you know what gravity looks like?

What?

Gravity, things falling down.

No. Maybe like an apple? Or a falling plane?

Or a fat man on a trampoline?

Maybe. What about you? Are you Buddhist?

Was Buddha Buddhist? Batukhan asked me.

He didn't even know he was Buddha.

What did the Buddha say about the world? he asked me.

He said that our actions lead to consequences.

No, he didn't say that. All that was only made up later.
What he really said was all this is a smokescreen. We're
thrashing around in a giant pool of shit, hoping to convert
some of this eternal shit into wine.

I never heard that part.

Everything comes from nothing, and returns to nothing.

Okay, that sounds familiar. But I'm no expert.

So what the Buddha said was: there is no consequence of
anything. So there is no point having a choice either. All
choices mean nothing. Or every choice means the same
thing.

Maybe. I don't know, I said. There's no point thinking about
what someone said 2,000 years ago.

No, there isn't.

Are you working in Rome? I asked him.

Batukhan doesn't need to work, Fede said.

I have some money, undeserved and unearned but mine
nonetheless, Batukhan added.

That's the best kind of money. So what do you do?

I travel, he said.

Where have you been?

I was in Lebanon in 2006.

What were you doing there?

I was listening to the war.

Listening to the war?

First the Hezbollah struck, they called it Operation Truthful Promise. And then Israel promised there would be painful consequences. I flew there at once (I was in Sierra Leone before this), the day before they blew out the Hariri Airport. I raced from Beirut to Tyre, where the Israelis were dropping bombs every five minutes. Rented a basement hotel room, lay down on the bed, and listened.

That sounds a little . . . crazy.

It was tough. There was no room service.

What were you listening for?

The rhythms of the bombs going off. It was the most beautifully synchronized sound I had ever heard. Do you know what each sound meant?

That people were dying?

That with each blast, people were finally given the answer to the question we all ask: what the hell am I doing here?

And you were just lying in bed the whole time?

No, that would have driven me crazy. I had brought my whisky, and I went for a walk every afternoon: bought kibbeh and baba ghanoush from the family next door. I often asked the lady how she managed to concentrate with all the bombs going off. She said she listed to Beyoncé to drown out the sound.

And what're you doing in Rome?

I'm watching a football game.

What's your plan here?

Watch the Roma-Lazio game, get a beer.

I mean your long-term plan.

In the long-term, I'm planning on dying. What about you?

This whole place is filled with crazies. I looked up at the screen. Batukhan twisted his glass around on the table. He wasn't really watching. I saw him eye the English people in the bar a couple of times. Tottenham were playing Roma in the Champions League next week and the city was already reeking of white trash. (What? They're racist all the time, have you seen the treatment a black player gets on a football pitch in Europe. In India, we love a foreign team; you'd never see that kind of behavior in South Asia. We only brutalize and oppress our own people, never a gora white guy. But an Indian is always pretty fucking racist when it comes to anyone with a darker skin tone. I think I'll stop my stereotyping antiracist rant here.) There were about twenty of them. The types who would tear their shirts off at matches and throw down flaming chairs. And there were fifty-odd Italians. I like the Italians: you have some hoodlum-fascist types, but they don't usually hulk around town causing trouble, indisputably proving primate evolution.

What have you bet? I asked Fede.

If Roma wins, I'm marrying her.

If Roma wins, I'm getting another lover, Laura said.

And if Roma loses, I think I'll leave Rome. I've had enough of this city, Fede added. What about you?

I didn't have anything to bet. If Roma wins the Serie A this year, I'll catch up with the few guys in my office and we'll go for a beer. We'll talk about how Totti pulled off that free kick and how Batistuta was the best ever (many won't agree). They'll talk about how they want some Indian food. I'll say it's such a pity we don't get dosas in Rome. I'll meet Liesbeth and the gang for the weekend, we'll get stoned out of our balls (or uteruses) and shake our limbs in a half-lit hall with 300 other people. Then I'll catch the metro to work and look at a woman on her iPod and a man who's reading *La Repubblica* and nodding his head because this country's going to the dogs and I'll see young unemployed guys who fold their scarves with a triangle pointing downwards and are plotting to burn cars during the next protest. I'll see half-done buildings and graffiti and pizzerias that don't open in the mornings and cafés with people standing at the counter ordering their macchiato and *lungo*. I'll see long coats at the metro platforms filled out with people who will all be wishing they weren't there but when the train is late, they'll curse and sigh and raise their hands in anger.

If Roma loses, I'll meet the guys and we'll bitch about Totti's captaincy and we'll agree that he should retire now, though one of us will say he's still a legend. I'll walk down Via del Corso and see giant women with little dogs peeping out of their handbags and older men in perfectly tailored suits strutting down the road and the young Goths who meet in Piazza del Popolo with their eyes painted and their silver chains hanging in crescents from their pockets to their waists and I'll see people in metros who rush to the next available seat and the crowds in the planes who clap each time the plane lands and Italians everywhere twisting their forks into their carbonara and their amatriciana and their arrabiata. I'll see the girls in puffy jackets and the guys with their gold chains and men in corners with their necks turning around and women with straightened hair typing into their phones. I'll see half-finished buildings and garages with dead scooters and cats walking through the ruins. I'll see books reading people and TVs watching over families. And then I'll say I wish they had dosas in Rome.

Maicon foiled another attack at the back, leaping into his tackle. Roma were a goal up; and their defenders weren't allowing the Lazio forwards any space.

This is terrific, isn't it? Batukhan asked me.

Yes, it is. But Klose can always slip in a goal. He's some kind of genius, isn't he? But like an everyday working-man genius.

He's just another sneaky Lazio striker. They never man up and volley down the pitch. They always try their slimy shimmies down the left; win a free kick on a fake injury.

Is this a normal game? Batukhan asked Fede.

Depends on how you define normal.

Batukhan stood up and stretched his arms to the roof. He curled his torso around, limbering up as if he was going in to play.

Normal is when you see it coming, he leaned over and told me. When you see your whole life rushing towards you, like an oncoming train. And you're tied to the tracks.

Keita fell to the ground, clutching his ankle. But then the medics rushed in with a stretcher and carried him out. That wasn't normal.

That's why we let the game decide for us, Batukhan hissed into my ears. Then you're driving the train. You know exactly where it's going. Even if it's diving over a cliff.

He straightened himself and walked over to the group of English rowdies.

Hey, he said gently. They turned their backs to him.

HEY. What're you WANKERS doing in OUR town? Now he was screaming.

One of the men turned sideways towards Batukhan.

Batukhan pulled out his arm like a whiplash and drove a penknife into the man's hips.

The bar exploded. Batukhan turned to me and smiled: You didn't see that coming, did you?

When he turned his head back, a fist hammered into his face and sent it rocketing into the side of the bar. Batukhan collapsed on the ground.

Okay, let's go. Fede pulled me towards the kitchen. We're getting out of here. He yelled to Laura who slowly lifted her jacket. I followed, stumbling over chairs, crushing beer glasses on the floor, making way for the kitchen staff who were racing out with their meat cutters and rolling pins, screaming Dai Daiii Daiiiii. I looked back between the swinging doors and saw Batukhan ramming headfirst into a punk and hurtling both their bodies over the bar. The air was filled with chains, knives, and chair legs crashing into skulls, diving into bellies. The kitchen was empty and we walked out into the back alley.

That's so Roman, the knife to the ass. I can't take that shit anymore, Fede said. He leaned against a wall and raised the whisky to his lips. He still had his glass with him. This is why I'm moving to Sicily. Violence should be an act of art, not of stupidity.

I said bye to them and walked back. Then the skies split open and it started pouring. I waited under a parapet that was draped with angels pissing out rain at the edges. The walls wept with their black paint. Bangladeshi vendors scrambled out of corners, their hands filled with umbrellas for sale. Smokers outside bars threw their cigarettes at the cobblestones and rushed in.

Apparently the gods watch us all the time.

Allah scratched his nose.

Ganesha tried some modern art with his snout.

Jesus shrugged.

READING LINES

I read a story last night. And I thought of you.

Where did you read the story? Chiara was scooping out the froth from her cappuccino.

In a dream.

You read in your dreams?

No. Okay, I read it on the Internet. I thought it would be more evocative if I said I dreamed the story. Someone else put it up. But now that I'm saying it to you, I suppose it's my story too.

What is the story? she asked me.

One day you wake up and your nipples have disappeared. No scar, no groove, just flat, smooth skin. And then when you leave your bedroom your phone rings and you find out your father died the previous night. When your nipples don't return for a week, you realise what had happened. Your whole life, while you were sleeping, your father would sneak into your room and suck on your breasts to give you two enormous hickeys that you thought were your nipples.

Chiara continued licking her spoon.

And your father did it not because of any sexual urges, but because he just wanted you to feel normal. That was his sacrifice: giving you nipples.

This is your dream?

No, I told you. I read it on the Internet.

But the Internet is our dream now.

Maybe it is our collective dream. And someday it will come alive.

I read a story about you too. Chiara put her spoon down.

Where?

I read it at the same place.

Then how do you know it's about me?

If the story fits, then it's your story. Stories are not custom-made. If you feel like it is your tale, then it is yours.

What did you read about me?

Your mother died and you were really upset. In fact you were going hysterical with grief, throwing yourself on the ground, beating your chest and howling like a wolf. Your relatives were worried about you. So an old uncle gave you something from his medicine bag to relax. But he had Alzheimer's so it turns out he gave you Viagra. And then you had an uncontrollable erection. And the more you grieved, the larger your hard-on got. Till it was a huge tower, bigger than the rest of your life. You were pinned under the tower and they couldn't cremate your mother's body because she was stuck under you.

Do you always specialize in fairy tales? I asked her.

Yes, I had called Chiara back. I figured there was no point staying away. So, we met for a coffee. Then we headed to San Calisto for a couple of beers. She wore a full jacket, though it was quite warm that evening. But she had to: her broken life is for display on her arms.

San Calisto was the cheapest place in Rome. It's right at the bottom of the barrel in terms of fanciness. Which also means you get to see the dregs of the city. And people who don't need much light. Grab a drink, get hold of one of the plastic chairs strewn around the front and in five minutes you'll have a freak join you. If you aren't one yourself. A poet with a feather in his hat joined us. He read us his poetry. The poem was in Italian. I said I was Indian; and he said so was he and pointed to his feather. Then he read his stuff in stumbling English. He was about sixty. He had written a really good poem when he was eighteen. We both said we loved it. And then he insisted on reading more. Everything else was crap. He wrote about dark valleys and souls with no light and how he hated God and he was one of God's abandoned children. Chiara asked him to leave. He said fuck you to her, and then to me as well. Chiara said he should have died before twenty, in which case she might have liked him. He said he did die at twenty. Since then, he's been waiting to be buried.

He asked me for a drink. I gave him some money for a grappa, so he'd leave us alone.

And then we were alone. At the bottom of the barrel. We didn't need much light. Anyway the place didn't have any lighting. We were lit up by joints all around us, like fireflies in the savannah (do they have fireflies in the savannah?).

What have you been up to? Chiara said.

Nothing much. I have an office report to work on. Went out a few times.

Have you jerked off recently?

Not very often. Couple of times a week.

What did you think about?

Thought about you once.

What were we doing?

We were stranded in an airport, I think it was Frankfurt, we had both missed our flights (separate flights: you to Rome, me to Delhi). And we were arguing with the airline staff.

Are all your sexual fantasies stories?

All fantasies are stories.

What happened next?

You asked me a tautological pseudophilosophical question and I lost all interest in banging you. So I left the airport and took the train instead.

She laughed. A man in a large woolen shawl behind her laughed as well for no reason; her laughter was as infectious as cholera in a sewer pipe. In front of us, a Bangladeshi immigrant played out some magic tricks. I had seen the guy before. He started swallowing a sword. Deeper and deeper it went. He started screaming, waving his arms in the air, just the handle of the sword sticking out of his mouth. The crowd applauded. *Bravo, bravo caro, e pazzo.* Yes, he was crazy. And then he sent around an upturned hat through the chairs for us to drop our coins. Chiara pulled out a fistful of small change and dunked it into the hat. She was happy. Maybe we all can be. Sometimes the story demands it, and then we have to smile.

This is a fairy tale.

We went back to Chiara's place. And we had sex. Yes, however you define it, Bill Clinton or Hugh Hefner style, we had sex. Which was good.

She wasn't looking away. I wanted to, but didn't.

When we were done, I was lying next to her. She told me about her writing. She said she wrote only for herself. And for Marco. I had got used to Marco being the main deal in her life. I was okay being subsidiary. I felt like I was incidental in my own life. She said Marco was her reader. He read all her work. And he read her, all the time. She said she would send me some of her writing. But I shouldn't comment. Or reply.

I said I could send her my report. That's the most significant piece of writing I've ever done.

She didn't have anything more to say. We didn't speak. I could feel the little island of the bed flooded with our silence.

I felt very alone. But it was nice to be alone with someone.

She gripped my fingers and ran them down her arm slowly. I could feel the grooved highway of her life. The slit-lines ran from below the elbow all the way to the wrist. Some were smooth and straight and my fingers knew exactly where the wound began and where it ended. Some were a rash of angry strokes and I couldn't tell one from the other. When my fingers reached her wrist, she started pulling them back up her forearm.

She wanted me to read her lines.

But I didn't even know my own lines. How could I read hers?

Why? I asked her. Because you wanted to die?

No. Because I wanted to feel.

CAKE OR DEATH

OR

YOUTUBE DREAMING

On YouTube, a big man wearing a dress—a cross between a kimono and a cocktail outfit—and perched on high heels asked me: Would you like cake or death?

Cake, I said.

He wasn't pleased, so he asked again. Cake or death. And I repeated my answer.

Then he was in my living room. His name was Eddie (it was written on his bra straps; I couldn't see his bra, but he told me it was written on his bra straps). He said his question was rhetorical, because he had neither cake nor death to offer me. He had thought of being a baker at some point in his life, but his mother held the opinion that it didn't suit a man to bake cakes for a living; it didn't fit in with existing or foreseeably altered gender roles. So he started cross-dressing instead. His mom thought that was cute.

Eddie didn't make much sense.

I asked him anyway if I could choose only death. Is there no cake on offer?

Eddie said death is not on offer either. It's an all-or-nothing choice.

What would that mean? All or nothing of death?

You get all of death or you get nothing of death.

What's the difference?

There is none. We haven't figured out a way to measure death yet. It's always larger than life because way more people and animals and sentient beings have died than are alive at the moment. But all of us doing the measuring are alive and have no experience or knowledge of death. But again, everything that is alive now will be dead, so life is just a subset of death. He drew a diagram on my tablecloth (he had one of those Magic Marker pens).

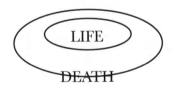

But then he contradicted himself. He said death consists of absolutely nothing at the same time, because where death is, nothing else is.

Where's death? I asked him.

It's not there.

So what do we do about it?

About death? Eddie asked. He was getting a little impatient.

Yes, about death. That's all I'm concerned with. I'm not interested in your stupid cakes.

You can't be interested in death. It's like being interested in a pink elephant that's practicing its salsa moves on Jupiter. It's just not there.

I've heard a similar argument before, I told Eddie.

Where could you have heard that?

Someone was explaining God, and said God is like a teapot in orbit around the earth.

You heard me. You heard what I have to say. All I can do is offer you cake. Do you want strawberry or warm chocolate?

Could I have both?

I'll make it happen. If you'll make it happen. I'm in your book.

When Eddie served me my second piece of cake, he said something that truly terrified me:

When you die, no one will remember your memories.

I asked him for a third piece: blueberry cheesecake. I needed some after hearing that line about my memories.

Chiara's Conversations with Ghosts

From: Chiara <chiara.camagni@gmail.com>

Date: Fri, Sep 21, 2012 at 3:41 PM

Subject: Conversations with Bolano

To: krantik.b@gmail.com

Hey K, so this is what I was talking about. My conversations with Bolano. This is the first message I sent to Roberto Bolano's Facebook page:

"Dear Mr Bolano

I have read, and enjoyed, a lot of your writing. I am a writer too, but not as successful or as brilliant as I would have liked.

Last year, my mother killed herself. I had to carry her to the hospital. But we couldn't save her. I have found that my narrative has broken down since then. I am also with a partner I love deeply (he's in London and I'm in Rome), but we don't know how to show our love. We think freedom is love. Maybe it is . . .

I am working on a text (don't know what to call it—novel/ memoir/ rant) on suicide and storytelling and narratives. I think writing this has helped me find some disjointed/ crazy way to think and speak again. I found this escape partly through your style and imagery.

I have finished 15,000 words. I will keep writing. But I don't think I'll show it to anyone.

Thank you for your books.

Warm wishes

Chiara

Maybe love is for the ones who suffer, the ones who know there is no warm light at the end. Who revel in the slow burn of their decaying flesh."

And then I sent a second message:

"And, of course, since you are dead, you will probably never read this. And since you died before Facebook, even your ghost won't.

But I thought I would just acknowledge your presence in my writing. That's it. Thanks."

I initially thought the above two messages were symptom-
atic of me going crazy. Then I realized the messages might
have been pointless, but at least they were self-aware.

I talk to ghosts a lot. So why not Bolano?

And then the ghost of Bolano replied.

"Un gran abrazo, Chiara. Muchas suerte."

Anyway, that's it. I think I'm done talking to Bolano.

From: Chiara <chiara.camagni@gmail.com>

Date: Fri, Sep 21, 2012 at 11:13 PM

Subject: Story

To: krantik.b@gmail.com

And this is the story I had started. I have no idea what to do
with it. Maybe I'll just let it be, let it stew in its incomplete-
ness. The protagonist's name is mine. I hope that's not too
distracting. Or maybe that is the whole point. Here goes:

Chiara's world had filled with sorrow, like water in an aquar-
ium, but she did not feel it because she had also grown gills.
Does a fish know what water is or what swimming feels like?

One day she found the words and told her friend Giovanna just how she felt. She said: I feel like I am surrounded by sorrow, but the sorrow is like water and I am a fish, so I don't really know what sorrow feels like.

David Foster Wallace already said that. But he wasn't talking about sorrow. He was talking about life, Giovanna said.

Chiara wanted to say: Did David Foster Wallace have any idea when he spoke about fish and water? But, if you have read that essay, you should also know that he borrowed the imagery from a Zen poet. Are they even called Zen poets? That sounds like some brand name to me. Max Mara Handbag for 200 euros, Zen poet on hire for fifty euros (poet offer does not include handbag). If I feel that way, and I just borrowed the word water from DFW, does that mean I don't know what the heaviness of sorrow feels like? Do you know what it feels like to be choking all the time? To dream of escape, but to have nowhere to go?

But instead, Chiara said: I haven't read *Infinite Jest*. I thought it would be too distracting.

Why would it be distracting?

All his little tricks, all those footnotes and flourishes, his bandana, is that all there is? What is he trying to say?

You have to read him to find out, Giovanna said.

Chiara wanted to smack her. Not because of what Giovanna said, but because she poked the air with her fork when she said it.

Why do we take these suicidal writers so seriously? Foster Wallace, Hemingway, Plath, Woolf. You know what I think: if they rejected life so viciously, there's something they know about it that we don't.

You just said you haven't read DFW. And you find him too distracting. How could you take him seriously?

I still take him seriously. I just find his writing distracting.

Right, because you knew what he was really like. Besides his writing, which was just a minor distraction? Giovanna raised her exasperated fork again.

Chiara said she had a meeting (they were at the cafeteria in office), one she had just remembered. She scooped up her tray and left. She deposited her unfinished meal on the little conveyor belt that carried trays away to die and walked to the elevator. She kept her eyes on the checked floor–black, white, and grey—floating below her and listened. What was she listening for? For something inside her, a thin quiet voice that could say: I am . . . I am . . . I am.

There was no voice.

In her office, she had a bell jar (not the book *The Bell Jar*, but she had an actual bell jar). The jar had three seeds of NERICA: the new rice variety she had helped develop and that had transformed food security sustainability across at least twenty countries. But now it held no appeal for her, not even as a frayed reminder of past achievements. She wasn't very old, not yet of the age that kicks back and reflects on "past achievements": she was in her late thirties and at the peak of her professional career, a description crafted for people who wish to see careers as peaks and troughs and accomplishments. That would have included most of her colleagues, but not Chiara. She only saw her career and her work as a constant churning: swallowing time and space and emotions and effort and spitting out reports.

We heard, from unconfirmed sources, that after lunch, Chiara went to the office terrace. She smoked one cigarette and then promptly sent another up in smoke to join its sister.

NOTES FOR THE STORY: Chiara walked over the parapet. Facing the question she first stumbled upon when she was fifteen, with a blunt knife and clumsy hands. Will it ever get better? The knowledge of dying alone. The knowledge of sorrow. The answer is unfortunately not. What could she do? Cast this knowledge, this "knowing that the darkness never ends," over the world. See how it refracts the sunlight.

She decided to grow her wings and fly away.

From: Chiara <chiara.camagni@gmail.com>

Date: Sat, Sep 29, 2012 at 2:27 AM

Subject: Midnight Soliloquy

To: krantik.b@gmail.com

I am in bed. I lie awake for hours. I am in the exclusive club that looks awfully fashionable from the outside, but no one in here wishes for membership: the world of incurable insomniacs. I could be dramatic and tell you this has only happened in the last few months, since what I call the upheaval in my life. But that's not true. I could also conjure a romantic air about the condition and say words rescue me when I am betrayed by sleep, but that is just nonsense. Usually there is only a low-grade headache, soreness in the limbs, a feigned stillness that is not sleep but only the wait for sleep. All of this sounds exotic. But it's just fucking annoying. Nothing that is true ever sounds pretty.

But tonight I am writing. I am typing this out in bed on my iPhone, because I'm too scared to walk all the way to the living room and get on my laptop, scared that I may plunge into a rabbit hole of endless links and Google searches and reddit conversations, all of which will be lost to my memory the next morning.

I don't sleep because I can't. I can't sleep because I don't.

I shut my eyes, pretending to be asleep, knowing I am not. I see the nondarkness that we mistakenly call black inside my eyes. I breathe steadily and will myself to sleep. And then I see her. My mother. Mamma. She had a voice like Rino Gaetano. (Who doesn't grieve for Rino Gaetano and his wizard voice, silenced at thirty by the monstrous stupidity of Rome? He didn't have a single enemy in the world, but now he's as dead as Tupac.) Mamma would sing all night: Gianna Gianna Gianna. Gianna and her magic touch with truffle, how Gianna never believed in music or in UFOs, Gianna had a crocodile, Gianna wanted the doctor, but he's not there. Gianna walks away when she pleases.

I remember parties where she would stay out on the terrace, even after dinner had been served and the guests had all gone inside the house. She was a voice in the dark.

She was also on the terrace when she killed herself. In the dark.

In my nonsleep, I feel sad. Very sad.

Though I am still not asleep, I will set my alarm fifteen minutes earlier for the morning. I will try and catch the metro earlier than normal. I will have fifteen minutes to spare before office. I will order a cappuccino from the bar near office, and then look out into an autumn morning and wonder about the people rushing to play out the rest of their lives.

I will smile. Tomorrow morning, I will be happy.

Sent from my iPhone

From: Chiara <chiara.camagni@gmail.com>

Date: Sun, Sep 30, 2012 at 7:08 PM

Subject: Trees that sway like ballerinas

To: krantik.b@gmail.com

Sometimes I sit still and allow thoughts and images to float into my head. Here are some:

Thought: When I write down a phrase like "my mother walked up a terrace and shot herself in the head and I have no idea why," I refuse to let the words speak to me, to evoke an emotion. I just type them out. And they are dead the moment they appear on the screen.

Nonthoughts/ images: In a room filled with sun, a young woman looks out of the window at trees that are swollen with green and rust-red leaves and sway in the spring wind like ballerinas. The woman is also writing and does not like the use of the word ballerina. But she lets it stay because, for the time being, it reminds her of paintings she had seen in a museum that evoked something similar to joy. The painting was of young girls lining up at a ballet class. It was probably by Degas.

The woman who writes about herself in the third person thinks of other paintings and, at this moment, comes up with nothing. There is a quiet melancholy that invades her. It is time to start shutting down and she lets images slowly creep into her mind and fade away. They include:

- A group of young women and men playing ping-pong under floodlights, slightly drunk on amaro and red wine, and thinking that this is life.
- A poet joins them for two games because he feels it may be a more honest use of his time than all the lines he has strung together. The poet is upset about mediocre novelists that earn more money and fame than brilliant poets. The poet loses both games of ping-pong.
- Many years ago, one of the players was a child and took table tennis classes. She learned the backhand

really well. She found a young boy with whom she kept practising her shots, with long rhythmic volleys across the shining tables, their edges snatching the light from the high windows. The player has forgotten the name and the face of the boy. She remembers the sweeping arcs of his forehand, like retaining the brushstrokes without recalling the painting.

There is a child outside with a gelato and I can hear his excited cries. His screams are wheeling in the sky above him with seagulls. There is a life to be lived. Then there will be nothing: no seagulls, no trees, no memories, and no record of what we were.

From: Chiara <chiara.camagni@gmail.com>

Date: Sun, Sep 30, 2012 at 11:23 PM

Subject: RE: Trees that sway like ballerinas

To: krantik.b@gmail.com

I don't know why I'm sending you these e-mails. All of this is none of your business.

WILD PIGS

The next day, as I was getting into work, I got a call. There was no number, so I figured it might be Vineet, Pooja's brother. I halted the sliding doors, jumped in, jumped out, gave them an existential crisis, and then leaped out of the building. An actor with no lines cannot fail.

I picked up and kept quiet.

Krantik?

Hi, Vineet. What's up?

Don't what's up me, you bastard.

Always great to talk to you too.

You pushed her to the edge. She said she was talking to you and then she went and jumped into the canal.

Did you ask her what we were talking about?

No, I didn't. But you knew she was in a mess. You called her to Amsterdam and then you guys shared a room.

Yes, we did. I didn't trick her into coming, Vineet. She wanted to go to Amsterdam. And I wanted to meet her.

And she visited you in Rome. We find a good family like yours and you turn out to be such a fucking lowlife.

Vineet, you need to calm down.

Calm down? You've ruined my sister's life, and you're telling me to calm down! She told me you're not even a manager. You're still a management trainee. A druggie, a failure, and a liar.

Vineet, I think it's time you stopped blaming me. Or her. Also time you stopped trying to get her married off.

What do you mean? You're coming in June next year and you're marrying her.

Who said anything about marrying her? I don't think I'm ready. I don't think she's ready.

If you came from a family like ours, you'd know what your word meant.

If I came from a family like yours, I'd also be blind. Because my head would be up my ass.

Krantik, you need to shut up now. But you see, beta, you're engaged to her, and if you back off now, terrible things might start happening.

What terrible things? Don't talk bullshit, Vineet.

Things happen, Krantik. All the time. And you know, Papa's an MP. He's expected to even become a Minister of State in the next cabinet. We cannot lose face over this whole mess you've created. And ministers can make things happen. To you, to your mom.

I saw people moving in and out of the sliding doors, obeying the doors, taking one step after the next and walking into the building. I didn't want to think about Ma. And now my heart was slamming against my chest. I could feel a lightning bolt of pain shoot through every joint and every synapse in my body.

I'll tell you a few more things that can happen, Vineet. A newly appointed minister can be suddenly exposed as a paedophile. Not just child porn, years of abusing his own son. Who's turned out so screwed up in the head he's enabling his father's illegal activities.

What the fuck are you talking about?

You know what I'm talking about: your dad whose balls you have sucked for the entire duration of your miserable existence.

That's not even true. What the hell . . .

Who cares if it's true? You threaten me with your goons, and you think I'll wait for you, bent over, pulling my own ass open? I went to IIT Chennai and the people I smoked up with, my fellow miserable druggie friends, were all studying in the Asian College of Journalism. You call me once more and we'll make sure this story breaks.

You asshole. You can't just make up stuff, you piece of shit.

Of course, I can. We all make up our lives. Be very careful, otherwise I'll make up yours. You have way too much to lose.

You're crazy. Bat-shit crazy . . .

I'm crazy? I'm CRAZY? You miserable fucking piece of dog-cum. Bhenchod, Maa ke Laude, Madarchod. If you piss me off, you'd better get someone to kill me right now. Because I'm empty inside and if you don't watch out, the only thing I'll do for the rest of my life is harbour the seeds of your destruction. If you don't kill me in the next two days, I'll train wild pigs for the next twenty years to come and eat you alive.

What the . . .

They'll hunt down your family, just you and your dad. Not Pooja.

Who?

The wild pigs I'll train.

And then I hung up.

By the time I got into the lift, I could barely breathe. There were voices all around me. How was the weekend? Did you see the match? I was tired of them all. So I thought of some of my favourite things. The song I mean, but I forgot the lyrics. So I made some up.

Girls in white dresses and blue satin sashes.

Smiling cute faces and large group pictures.

All good friends are posing for Facebook.

Pizza and vino in Instagram fashion.

Look at my pasta, isn't it pretty?

Raindrops on roses and whiskers on kittens.

This wasn't working. So I practised my Italian in my head:

Tutto mondo è pazzo, tutti è cazzo.

And then some conjugations: *palaconto, palacontiamo, palaconte.*

I can imagine Vineet in his swanky office, trying not to get worked up. He adjusts his tie, makes sure the end falls pat in the middle of his belt buckle. Will he call Papa? Not yet, wait till dinner and family time. And then he slithers to the office coffee machine and steams out a cup. His assistant's typing and he's looking at her breasts, wishing they were smothered under his hands. And then he starts tapping the coffee counter because he can't wait to see me dead. Or paralysed at least. What he doesn't know is that cells inside him are slowly losing the ability to divide. His body is in a stable, relatively constant condition. But it's falling apart. Every day 150,000 people die. And they can't help it. Vineet thinks he's ahead. But he's just in a queue.

I get to my desk. Claudia says hello and she's got new earrings. Do I like them? We spend ten hours three feet away from each other every day. The wall in the middle isn't high enough. We spend 9.5 hours making sure we don't look at each other.

Yes, those are lovely.

I'm thinking of Buddha hands, index finger and thumb joined and the other fingers fluttering into an open petal. I'm thinking of Vishnu chilling on his serpent bed and Shiva doing a bong. Jesus is sitting by a lake cutting his toenails. Damned desert dust.

I switch on my system. Everything takes too fucking long. The radiation from your TV: 1 percent of that is from the original Big Bang. Yes, even that's not over yet. On my desktop, in the middle of a Camel Lights blue screen, a darker circle slowly unwinds. Fuck Vineet and his dad. I could call my journalist friends if I wanted. And his dad looked like a paedophile anyway. Or maybe I'll just say he tried to molest me.

I breathe deep. I need some peace. I have to forget where I am. First I have to rid myself of attachments. The iPhone goes out first. Then my Kindle, then the Bosch painting print I carry around to different places just so people who visit know my obscure taste in art. Then those stupid African sculptures. Get rid of the Foucault books on the shelf;

I never managed to read beyond chapter two anyway. If I put everything I own into a container and ship it to Aruba, along with everything I've ever read and all the music I've heard, what would be left behind?

I don't need any memories. You know, that school quiz, that kiss on a swing (I was only twelve), the terror of my first hard-on, the first time I got stoned and the walk back home stretched forever and ever, or that party after which Mohsin and I were lying in bed together and he leaned over (anyway, forget I just said that), my dad and his model cars . . .

Markus was standing in front of me. One strand of hair had escaped the tenacious hold of his gel and pointed down, slicing his forehead in two.

RISE and SHINE. How're we doing on the report?

It's going okay. Some of the numbers are difficult to generate, but I'm working on them.

You remember what I said? We need to show a 30 percent increase in our efficiency. If we haven't been efficient enough, it means we've got some slack around here. If we have slack, we have to tighten our belts. And I can see a little flab in front of me right now. May need liposuction.

Yes, Markus. I think we have achieved thirty.

You know where they dump liposuction fat? It becomes medical waste, forgotten forever. You don't want to be discarded liposuction fat, do you?

No, I don't.

I read that in *Fight Club*.

Cool book. I smiled. If I have no memories, I won't remember what makes me happy. Then there'll be no need to smile.

The magic number is 30 percent, Markus said. I'm relying on you. The first rule of my club is you meet your targets.

I'm trying, Markus. I think we'll make it.

What's the second rule? he asks me.

The second rule is I have to meet my targets.

You're a bright kid. I want the report by COB today since you're on leave tomorrow. Or you'll be a bright, unemployed kid.

Do turtles remember the sea? Even if they've spent their whole lives on a terrace?

Do they ever wish they could leap off? What if we could get rid of all our regrets? Would that make us lighter? Maybe we could achieve buoyant flight, like those snakes that float from the treetops. Imagine if all of us leaped out of our office windows, our arms spread-eagled, floating to the ground, like a flock of geese heading south. Wave after wave, we would kick off from the edges of our steel and glass towers.

I clicked on the data set I had collected. I had files that linked to other back-end files and then all I had to do was run the final analyses on two or three main interface sheets and we could get the results for the entire portfolio. 30 percent, 30 percent, that's what I'm looking for.

The Ghana office improved their processing time by 12 percent, they increased their customer base by 7 percent.

I don't remember more than 60 percent of my life.

The Austria team improved their customer retention by 54 percent; I need to factor in a multiplier of 0.35 on retention.

Ninety percent of the world is wishing they were with someone else, wishing they were somewhere else, that they were someone else. If all of them switched places, they would still be wishing for the same things.

The India office increased their customer base by 67 percent, but increased their product-loan disbursement by only 23 percent. The India office also saw a decline in their recovery of 5 percent.

Ninety-nine percent of us identify ourselves by our given names. But that's not even who we are.

The Vietnam office reduced their effectiveness time by 15 percent; their outcome indicators show an enhanced performance of 7 percent.

I have spent 95 percent of my life doing things I didn't want to do. I never know what I want to do.

If we got rid of all our memories, would we also get rid of all our hopes?

Pooja didn't have too many aspirations in her life. She said she didn't have a soul either. She said Deepak Chopra created the soul. When I first met her, with both of our families in their living room, she came out wearing a sari and carrying a tray full of teacups for all of us. I thought I was condemned to a life of boredom. But I didn't mind. There isn't much that excites me. The whole world is on reddit and Facebook anyway.

But then she went back to London to finish her degree and suggested we should meet. We met in Rome and then in Amsterdam. She was a tea maker in a sari; but in jeans she was a stoner. We were sitting in a café, both trapped by the wishes of our families but reconciled to the rest of our lives. Or so I thought. Behind us, the tower of Amsterdam Central scratched the sky. She was bent over the table, her fingers flying over the paper. Drop, drop the roasted hash. Drop, drop. Sprinkle tobacco . . . split cigarette open, empty its belly out. She finished making the joint and slid it along her tongue. She held it up. This is triumph. I scratched the lighter on and burnt the twisted tip. We could have been great together. Dry, I needed some Sprite.

Sprite. Cold and silver, rushing down my throat, maybe that waitress can help. She smiles, tucks her hair behind her ears. It's razor-sharp blonde. Blonde is unreal. Touch? Don't need to.

Pooja says I shouldn't burn her if we end up staying together for a long time. I tell her about the cremations I have witnessed. Sometimes, when the fire is halfway through, the carcass sits up—the spine is twisted and props the head up. At least the face was charred through. If the mouth had smiled or said something, we would have all fainted. The helpers scramble around the pyre with iron rods and beat the body back on the wood. All is well again.

The dead need to stay well and truly dead. Only sometimes they should come back and sing Dylan.

Sprite, please. Heineken. Small, medium. The waitress tap-taps into a beeping pad; there must be numbers all in a row. No counting needed.

I suck on the joint. Pooja stretches her arms. In the middle of the V, her face splits into a smile. I don't know what love is. If I did, I could love her.

She looks happy. But she doesn't know what joy is.

We should walk, I hear my voice. Where? Bulldog café, sit near the canal. We start to move. Across the road, a crowd is waiting for their fries. Ten minutes for potato. Twenty minutes to walk from the fries shop to the Van Gogh Museum. Fifteen minutes to get the perfect family photo for Facebook. I think I'm thinking, but actually I'm talking. The day rolls out in front of me. And then the rest of my life. It will keep going on and on, like those Outlook calendars you can keep scrolling down.

And you don't want to scroll down the rest of your life? Now she's talking.

I don't have a choice, do I?

We sit down by the canal. This is good shit, isn't it? Yes, uh-huh, both heads nod. It's called Nepal Temple. Have you ever been there? No, I've only been to Darjeeling. Have you been to Bhutan? No, I've been to Assam.

We could go on forever. Again, it's me speaking. Have you been to Bogota? No, I've been to Paris.

She laughs. But it's a thin laugh, like she doesn't have too many to spare.

There's a boat on the canal. Women in hats, men in flowery shirts, one guy's holding up a trumpet, another's holding up a bong. They wave at people on the bridges.

Again I feel like I'm in a movie. I light another joint. The unfeeling protagonist. I tilt my chin. There is no mirror. Or the world is one. All the time. Inhale. Exhale with pursed lips. Turn away. I'm in a movie.

What do you think? she asks me. She orders two more beers.

This is nice.

No, I mean about us.

What about us?

We're stuck together aren't we, with our arranged marriage scene.

Looks like it, I said.

Would you like that?

It might be nice. And we both like some of the same things. I laugh.

What?

Nothing, you look pretty stoned.

Do I? She rubs her eyes.

What about you? I ask. Do you think this will work out, you and me?

I'm just so tired.

Yes, it's been a long day.

Every day is too long.

Would you rather be with someone else?

No.

Same here. I can't think of anyone. Then we're okay?

I guess. She takes the joint from my hand. You know, like an Outlook calendar, I just can't believe how much longer I have to go.

You don't have to go anywhere.

I mean, how long do I have to travel through time?

You're a time traveller?

We all are. We are born, then we live, and then we die.

She picks up a magazine. It has crumbs of weed sticking to it. Freida Pinto has some sticking out of her nose. Pooja points it out to me and laughs. One laugh less to spare.

What next? she asks me.

I don't know. I suppose we get married next year? Our families chose the groom and the bride, so they can choose the date as well.

Yes, they can. We can get married, we'll go seven times around the fire, throw some ghee into the flames. And then we'll go to Paris for our honeymoon. If we want to be exotic, we could go to Kenya. You'll get a promotion, I'll get a job, one of those creative types. Maybe marketing, even journalism. I'll break a story about corporate fraud or I'll launch a new product that'll capture 35 percent of the market.

What're you talking about?

About time travelling. And then you'll want a kid, or worse still I'll want a kid because we have a car and the backseat just seems so large. So you'll stop slipping on your condoms or I'll get off the pill. We'll have a child: Antara or Aarti? Abhimanyu or Arjun? Which do you prefer?

She keeps going on and on. The joint is over. I'm not annoyed, but I want her to stop talking about the future.

This is the life that happens to everyone, I say. You can't be, I don't know, Madonna or Frida Kahlo just because you think the ordinary is boring. Or you can be. You can start painting, you could start . . .

One day I'll be old and I'll feel my knees hurt. You'll be impotent or I'll be constantly tired. We would have had three and a half affairs each and lived in two cities for long periods of time.

Pooja, I say. I may say it a bit loudly. You don't have to marry me. I'm fine with that. I'm in no hurry. We can go back to our hotel room and I can pick up my stuff and leave.

It's not about you.

Then what is it? Dammit, I don't need this entire load.

It's about my whole life. Any life I think of is no different from any other.

That's not true.

I have always known it, she says. Even when I was a kid, I knew it. I should have just gone ahead in college and done it.

Done what?

Don't you see? She's talking with her mouth away from me. There is nothing inside and there is nothing in the end.

The joint had died in my hand. I want to say something. I want to say I agree. Maybe I say it. Maybe I say more: maybe I say that's true, and even if we're together, we'll never ever know each other, and I could never help her, but she wasn't expecting that anyway, was she? And there is only this life and these things that will fill our lives little by little, and we'll take all the stupid stuff and think we've done something real. And then one day it'll all come to a stop.

And that will be that.

Could you get the bill please? I'm not feeling too well, she says.

I step up and my body feels lighter at once. I walk to the bar, digging for the wallet in my pocket. Behind me, she ties her hair and walks to the canal.

I was in the smoking area behind the nonmetaphorical iron bars. I didn't call Massimo; usually we go for our smoking breaks together. There was another guy smoking: he was a big bearded chap who always dressed in suits and *Pulp Fiction*-style narrow black ties. Also had crooked teeth.

I went back to my files and started running the tests again. I'm good with numbers. My favourite is sixty-nine.

I also like seven: sins and dwarves.

Anyway. Time to get to 30 percent. If I didn't get this report like Markus wanted, during the next Looking Back, Leaping Forward session, he would make sure my balls were extracted out of the sack where they lie waiting for action.

Pooja was still sinking.

And I was looking for a stupid number.

Shit. I only got a 27 percent improvement.

I went down for another smoke. I couldn't go and tell Markus the numbers weren't adding up. That just wouldn't do. *Pulp Fiction* man was still smoking downstairs. I'd never spoken to him. Often seen him ordering a glass of milk in the café in the morning. A giant in a black suit drinking milk. He could be an assassin or a Mafia enforcer: drinks his glass of milk, pays his bill, leaves a tip, and then pulls out a shotgun and proceeds to erase all forms of life in the café.

Fuck. And now I would lose my job in what? Three months.

I tried processing the data again. The results just wouldn't change. I could round off a few percentages and get it up to 28 percent.

Are you on it? Markus keeps popping up, like a haemorrhoid.

Yes, absolutely.

And are we looking at 30 percent?

I think so.

I think so isn't good enough, Krantik. You're a professional. If I needed someone to guess what the numbers are like, I would have got an intern. Do you know how many people your age are earning your salary? I've told the MD we're getting thirty. Don't embarrass me.

Markus, we should have checked before promising our board.

Do we have a problem here? If you're not up to the task, let me know. There are enough people out there who can do your job.

No, there's no problem here.

Good. Because, you know, you Indians are good at doing tasks but not at taking responsibility. I want you to own this report. I want you to make this yours.

Absolutely. I love stereotypes that can cover a billion people.

All these numbers mean nothing. Every number is made up. Did Pooja count before jumping? One, two, and three, Go. Or did she count: 0.347, pi/3, root of 17, Go. Does Chiara count the lines she's carved on her arms? Is forty-seven worse than thirty-five?

And then I had only half an hour left. I was taking the next day off: I had to drink the stomach cleansing fluid that evening and shit everything out. And then I had the colonoscopy the next day. I had told Chiara about the test. She was worried, but I told her it was just a routine checkup. But it was nice she worried.

I needed to start emptying my guts out soon to prepare.

Fuck this shit. Markus wants thirty, he'll get thirty.

People should get what they want. Instagram pictures that look just like the 1920s, Facebook posts that all your friends like and most of them share (share this cute kid to stop napalm bombing in Peru, like this black man's picture—the guy wearing a beret cap—because he'll stop kidnapping kids then, share this potato for no reason), multiple orgasms without rabies and blow jobs from an androgynous Van Damme/Sharon Stone cyborg, climate change and polar bears in Central Park, rose petals kissed with morning dew, and Japanese men in gimp suits with Rihanna's underwear stuffed in their mouths.

So I changed the numbers. I hiked up the Ghana office performance (those guys need a break, Africa Rising and all) and the Vietnam office indicators (I love that monk who's sitting stone still while the fire swallows him whole, you've seen that crazy shit, right?).

And then I got 30. In fact I got 30.7 percent, just so it wouldn't be too precise. Markus can impale himself on his pyramids while jerking off to this.

Floss your teeth, Markus, you have 30 percent.

Flex your bicep, suck in your abs, you have 30 percent.

You have 30 percent, congratulations: now your dick is two inches longer.

I saved the file and mailed it.

Only the servers were down. So the mail stayed on my system with a Confucius circle spinning round and round. I put the file on a pen drive and went to his office. Markus's office, not Confucius's (do you put another s after an apostrophe? I have no idea).

He saw the main sheet with 30.7 in bold purple lettering (I like bright choices in font colour).

You're a rock star, did you know that?

I put my hands in my pocket, looking humble.

I mean, you're like the love child of Slash and Hendrix. That's how cool you are.

Is that from *Fight Club* too?

No, I made that up.

Cool.

Great stuff, Krantik. And perfect timing. I'm leaving soon, but I'll take this with me and go over it in the morning. This is why you're here. You're here and you're working with me because you are the future.

Thanks, Markus.

Have a fun break. Are you planning anything exciting?

No, the usual.

Aha, I know what that means. You'll be sniffing coke off a hot girl's boobs, won't you?

Something like that.

I packed my stuff (that included the super-laxatives for my colon cleansing).

Pooja was still sinking. And since she dived, it has felt like she's dragged me down too. Like I'm still tied to the bottom of the canal, too scared to set my feet down on the bottom, too weak to struggle and claw my way back to the top.

KIM KARDASHIAN

Purgatory. I don't really know what the word means. I mean there are all these words that I read and I don't really know what they mean. I always thought of purgatory as some kind of hellhole where you are stuck forever. But it also sounds like a place where you get purged. Cleaned out. Like an organic climate-positive wellness centre where you go to get your toxins flushed out.

Lugubrious. Again, I have no idea. Sounds like the soft-edged in-and-out swishing of a well-lubricated ass. I mean lubricated with some deluxe Durex product.

Saturnine. Sitting still while the world goes crazy around you. Sixth rock from the sun, you're so cool you even have rings around you like a whirling caravan of groupies.

Garrulous. Gables and ladies in dresses that bloom around their legs. Raising barns in Amish country in long hats.

Parsimonious. Just the right blend of spices. Pizza fresh off the wood oven and slicing straight and true under your knife.

Lemon. Lemonade. High as a kite. Heroin base.

Dichotomy. Castration.

I didn't know what it meant, but I knew where I was. Purgatory.

I had the colon-cleansing mixture in four large bottles in my fridge. Every fifteen minutes, I took a few swigs. And then I had to wait by the loo the whole evening. And I mean right next to the throne. Each volley of shit sent me crashing to the floor.

I chose a list of The Who songs to play on loop for a while: Pete Townshend's windmilling his guitar like a maniac and Daltrey's swinging his mike over the audience like a lasso.

Foetal. Curled, beginnings, endings.

I'm on the floor quivering. I'm being flushed out.

They say the moment before you die, your whole life flashes before your eyes. Unspooling, like a tape you can't play again. (I knew I wasn't dying. I sound dramatic, but I can be cold and calculating sometimes, totally plugged into what's happening, but creating alternative narratives because why the hell not.)

I don't know what's inside me. Tomorrow, the doctor will sedate me and turn me sideways and then slowly insert a long telescope pipe into my anus. It's ten feet long. Maybe only colonoscopy surgeons have seen the soul snuck away inside our intestines.

Is that it? The surgeon's assistant asks, bent over my curled body and peering into my ass. No, that's just his Facebook profile picture. See: he's holding a goblet of Belgian beer. Okay.

What's that? That's him in his office, note the dull reflection in his eyes: that's the life he had dreamed of.

Then they see Markus standing over me. Massimo talking about his dad. We are the generation that have lost our parents but have found Facebook, he says. We're smoking a joint, then we're in a club and we're jumping because the bass just got louder, our arms are in the air; then I'm on a plane and I'm a praying atheist because 5,000 tonnes of metal is climbing into the sky; then I'm at university and we're sitting around half-finished cups of coffee, someone's talking about a disastrous date, we're all laughing and leaning back against our chairs because our stomachs hurt; I'm holding tingling cricket bats and girls are standing around and watching; a walk in the rain with a girl who might like me but I don't like her; family dinners with the TV on and picnics with the radio playing Kishore Kumar; listening to Dylan while solid fingers pluck strings in front of me; my first fumbling kiss; and a fight with my sister when we were kids and we gave each other the evil eye for the next week.

They probe further and they see hopes that are painted yellow and mauve (what other colours could hopes be?) and fears in electric blue and temptations made of velvet and steak. They see my name. It's written in English then in Hindi and then in a language we can't read. Finally there's a sound we can't hear.

Massimo calls when I'm listing options for what lies up my bowels.

Hey, how's it going?

Okay, I've survived ten trips so far.

If it's any consolation, random foreigners have been driving their SUVs up my ass the last hour.

Why? What happened?

All the heads of the country teams are here to meet senior management. And guess who's preparing their presentations while they show their kids around the Vatican.

I'm lying on the bathroom floor. I'm clean, but I'm wiping the seat. (Don't look at me like that! Have you ever tried a colon-cleansing laxative and managed to time your expulsion to the exact second your ass is perched in the middle of your seat?)

What are the country heads presenting? I croak.

They're presenting their respective efficiency reports.

What? Which countries? Now I'm on my feet.

All of them. This is trouble.

Ghana? Vietnam?

Of course, I said all of them.

And they're presenting their own indicators to the bosses? I thought they were all covered in Markus's presentation.

That's what I heard. They'll all be doing their show, and then Markus will start his.

I ask Massimo to go and check the data on their presentations. I hold my breath while he looks. If Markus finds out I had made up the numbers, I'll be looking forward to the prospect of semipermanent unemployment. Massimo checks and yes, they have the actual figures, in bold red because they're so proud of their measly 10 percent improvements. I still hold my breath. Easier to control all bodily functions when you're not breathing. Long-distance divers don't fart.

I'm fucked, Massimo.

You mean besides your ten-foot anal probe tomorrow.

No, I mean I'm fucked like a five-year-old in MJ's bedroom.

I don't think MJ ever fucked a kid. I think he just never realised he had grown up. MJ was the Peter Pan of our generation.

I am being serious.

Hard to tell.

Okay, you can't say a word about this, but I made up some numbers on Markus's report. I hiked up the numbers for Ghana and Vietnam. I mean hiked them up to reach our 30 percent target.

Why the hell would you do that?

Because. Because he just went on and on about his 30 percent, and I had to leave, and he was crawling all over me. Because. I don't know. I was just too tired of all the bullshit. I thought if they want 30 percent and they want me to get 30 percent, then I'll just make it happen.

Don't you know we have an auditor's office? If he catches on, you're . . . fucked.

Yes, I am.

I go on Facebook. I always do that when I can't make sense of my life. Maybe in the middle of it all—the lopsided smiles and the duck faces and grilled meat with mashed potatoes on the side (in sepia tones because it happened so long ago we have another name for the time: it's called yesterday) and faces being ripped back by the wind in the middle of a skydive but the hand's still doing a thumbs-up and the inspirational quotes that you must share because surely you know someone who's autistic and needs your support—I'll find an answer.

If I am a mirror, who is looking in? Do I even care about this job? I don't even know. Or am I just making up all this bravado because I'm too scared to admit I care. How would I know? If I'm asking the questions, who can answer.

I go for another shit and this time it's firmly established that there's a World of Warcraft game being played out inside my intestines (have you seen the guy who freaks out because his WOW account is cancelled?). If I lose my job, I'll go back to India. I haven't learnt much in the last two years here, and India's a far more competitive job market than you could imagine. Only I'll never get a good reference from this place, so I'll probably end up working at McDonald's. Or as a male prostitute; I could take a gladiator uniform with me. Or I could spend the rest of my life playing video games and growing a thousand folds of fat into my mother's sofa. The American Dream might be closer than I think.

I can't have that happening to me. Also, you know what, fuck Markus. Fuck the system. They're all screwing us over. I'm not being the fall guy here. I could do the proper thing and mail Markus. Or call him and redo the presentation. But then it's a Roma game night. I'm going all in. So I call Federico.

Hey.

Fede, are you free?

Not really. Roma Napoli has just started. How come you're not here?

Because I'm not well. And I'm in trouble.

We're all in trouble. Roma was just massacred by AC Milan. Now I'm committed to a life of crime. Or returning to it. At least till the end of the season. That was my bet.

I tell him about Markus and my fake report.

So you didn't e-mail him? Just gave it to him on a pen drive?

Yes. I also guess that Markus left soon after me, so the only other copy of my report would be on his laptop (that he was taking home).

Do you have his address?

I can get it.

Cool. Don't worry. No biggie as we say in Cali. Meet me at the Colosseo metro at midnight.

Massimo gets me Markus's address from our company database. It's always good to have an IT friend. By midnight, I have drained myself completely. I haven't eaten the whole day, so there's a constant rumbling in my stomach. There are apparently a billion people who never get enough to eat (I remember from some UN reports, I read that kind of political shit too). An empty growling stomach must be the soundtrack to their lives, much like Lady Gaga or the Rolling Stones is to yours.

Federico is waiting at the metro station with a car. I climb in, and there's a huge cylinder in the backseat.

What's that?

That's the answer to your problem. Sleeping gas.

I don't know what the plan is. But at least he has one. And sleeping gas is not as scary as having a Kalashnikov or a rocket launcher in the backseat. Or Lindsay Lohan.

We're waiting outside the main door and Federico says he loves modern apartment buildings. So much easier to break into. How are we getting into the building? Don't worry, he says, Romans are the most trusting people in Europe. That's why I love this place. He rings a random buzzer. *Sono idraulico.* I'm the plumber. No questions asked. Door opens.

I'm on top of the building. Maybe I could check in on Foursquare? This scene is being plastered onto my soul: standing on the terrace of Markus's building, leaning over the air vents while he slips three pipes tonguing out of the cylinder into the different slits. I'm putting only his floor out. We'll have ten minutes. Here, wear this. Then we're wearing masks, like Bane, and waiting. Fede keeps checking his watch and doing a countdown with his fingers. But his countdown is not in sequence: three, seven, two, five, one, Go.

We walk down the stairs to Markus's floor and it's like a post-zombie building. TVs playing from doors, Italian anchors screaming inanities into drugged-out living rooms, someone's listening to Lady Gaga (to remind us, the gods are watching).

Fede stops at a couple of doors, slips out a little rod from his jacket and slides the grooved sharp end into the gap. He yanks the door open. But we don't enter. It's just to give the impression that more apartments have been broken into, he says. I don't know what Fede did in California, but he probably wasn't an accountant.

When they hear that his laptop was stolen, the neighbours will make something up too. Romans love pity.

We get to Markus's door and with a slip and a crack, we're inside.

The lights are on. Markus has a bright purple lava lamp in the living room floor. Blobs of lava float up and down, throwing twisted shadows all over the walls like a David Lynch movie wet dream. There's a zebra-striped rug on the floor. Fede stops at the lamp and starts unplugging it.

Hey, we just need the laptop.

You just need the laptop. I need this lamp.

No, Fede, let's just get the laptop and go. All I need is the report.

Go ahead, get your report.

I walk into the room. Markus is slumped on the floor next to his bed. He's wearing a pink lace dress; the bra straps can barely contain his chest muscles. His dress is ruffled and rises up to his waist. I can see half of a shaved nut. He's also pissed on himself, but that's the sleeping gas relaxing all his muscles.

Now I feel bad for him. Anyone wearing such a nice dress can't be too much of an asshole.

I look for the laptop but it's not on his reading table. I find his office bag and open it. The laptop is inside. There's also a photo. I pick it out. It's a photo of our office team. Maybe he actually likes his colleagues. Now I'm sick in the stomach. And then before I can lift the bag from the floor, I'm feeling really sick. No, this is not a metaphor. I need to use the loo. Fuck fuck, the laxative's not done with me yet. I can't leave: leaking a trail of shit for the cops to find us. I slam into the loo and collapse on the seat before it's too late.

I'm done quickly and I flush. I wash up and open the door.

And Markus is standing in front of me.

He's in some Shaolin Kung-Fu pose, his hands puckered into swans and raised above his head. But he's not steady: his eyes are quivering in their sockets and he can barely keep his legs straight.

It's YOU. You little cocksucker. *Haista vittu. Haista paska.* How DARE you? Then he's blabbering again, his hands are

unfolding slowly above his head as he prepares his death-
blow. Runkkari, you will suck my SHIT.

So I punch him. With everything I've got. And that includes
thirty years of never knowing exactly why I was where I
was. Of being stuck in the same spot while everything spins
around me.

I feel the nose bridge cracking. Markus, in slow motion,
keels over. Now he's on the floor with piss on his dress hem-
ming and blood dribbling out of his nose. I tilt his face
sideways so he doesn't drown in blood.

Fede hears the noise and walks in. I think he's laughing, but
I can't hear him because of the mask. I get the bag with
the laptop.

Now I have to run. Will Markus remember? Of course, he
will.

We get into Fede's car. I think of all the people in the building slowly coming to their senses, some won't even realise
they were sedated for ten minutes. No different from the
rest of their lives.

Will Markus call the police? Will he be too embarrassed
by the fact that I saw him in his dress? Should I call him?
Tonight? Or wait till morning? Will I get an early morning
visit from the special carabinieri police, shoving their semi-
automatic weapons into my mouth?

I thank Fede and get off near the Protestant cemetery (he
leaves with the laptop, the lava lamp, and his cylinder). I

don't care what Markus wears or what he does. I just don't want to be screwed over. Now it's like we've got each other by the balls. Only his are shaved, so they're difficult to hold on to.

I conducted an episode of assault and burglary. And he was just wearing a dress.

But he'd be too worried about what people at work thought.

I'm walking and, before I know it, I'm at Via Galvani. Making my way from the corner of dead poets to Chiara. It's late but she opens the door when I buzz; she sounds worried.

She's in a long nightshirt with Winnie the Pooh yawning into a starlit sky. Her hair is tousled into a crown around her head. If this were the only scene I remember during my moment-of-death-recap, it would definitely break my heart.

Are you okay?

Yes. In fact, I'm great.

What's happening? It's almost two in the morning.

I had to come and offer you the opportunity of a lifetime.

Krantik, if you're on something, please leave. I don't have the time for this. Not right now.

Can I come in? I have to talk to you.

If you're in trouble, then come in.

We're all in trouble.

She slouches on the sofa. I get myself a glass of water (I'm still empty inside) and I start.

Hear me out. I don't want to be here anymore. In fact, I don't want to be anywhere in particular.

Okay.

I lie a lot. I lie all the time. I don't mean the easy lies: investment fraud and drug deals and cheating spouses and disloyal friends. Those are the lies we deal out because we want to continue engaging with the real world, because we want to find something real in this world. But me, it's not just that I refuse to see. I make up all these worlds so I can't even see anything for real.

We all do, Krantik. Stop your juvenile obsessions with your-self and your privileged quests for something that will give you meaning.

I'm done with quests. But I have a plan. A real one. Have you heard of Goa?

I have. Krantik, are you okay? Or are you just fucking around?

There's this beach in Goa. It's called Palolem, hidden in the south. We could go there, you and me, and we could set

up a restaurant. I have some money, enough capital for a
shack. You could teach someone to cook Italian and I mean
the real thing.

What're you talking about?

I can cook too. You haven't tried my Thai curries. And I
could learn to make cocktails. Or you can take the bar if
you want, we'll work out the details.

You're fucking crazy.

This is the most serious I've ever been. It's not about the
food. We'll be away from all this. All of this, my job, your
stupid paintings, we don't need any of this shit.

You need to leave, Krantik.

Yes, I need to leave. And you need to leave. Come away,
this whole world is pulling us down. It's pulling me down.

You're pathetic. And now I'm serious. She sits up. You're
just like them all.

I'm pathetic? I come up with a plan, and I'm the one who's
pathetic?

Yes, you are. You're acting like a jerk right now.

Come with me, Chiara. You can do what you want. Marco
can come visit you. You'll be free. We'll have enough money
to get by, and that's all we need.

Listen. If this is how you behave, I don't want to see much of you.

You don't? She's really taking my trip now. What do you want to do instead? Sit here and slice up your arms, like you've done a thousand times before? Talk about your mom singing Gianna in the dark? Or spend your whole life grieving her gunshot?

Get out of my apartment. Get out, RIGHT NOW.

Of course, you don't want to hear me. Because you don't have the courage to examine this hippie-free-love life you've created. I know we'll be happy. That doesn't matter. We'll be free. Marco's just a dick in a sausage factory; they're making Spam for the whole world.

Shut up about Marco. This is not about Marco. She stands up and starts nudging me to the door.

No, it's not. I'm not moving. This is about you and me. How many more lines will you carve into yourself?

You're all the same. You fuck me once, I send you a few e-mails, and you think you own me. Maybe all you need is a wife.

I don't need a wife. I don't need anything. All I need is to get out of here alive. And so do you.

Now she's pushed me to the door. Have you seen yourself? she asks. You're so scared you can't even talk to real people. You spend your life asking directions from strangers.

I don't say anything, I can't say anything, but she carries on.

And you think a pain in your ass will kill you. You're too scared to live, and you're terrified of dying. And now you have a Bollywood plan to find love and life.

Now I'm outside the door and she slams it in front of me.

Go find your kitchen knife, I say, though I don't want to. That could help you feel better.

The door opens. She sticks her head out for a moment. Good your dad died so early. At least he didn't see you grow into this. Go home. Find another freak to talk to.

I walk back, empty trams run past me, but I can't be bothered to get on.

I put on some music, but I don't know what's playing.

I go to my bedroom and I pick up my cricket bat. I practise a few shots in the air, a cover drive with my arms above my head, a hook with my body swivelling on my toes.

And then I take guard near the oven.

I swing the bat back. A good back-lift is important for a powerful shot. I slam it into the oven door. The glass shatters into the dark space inside. I can hear the grilling trays clattering.

I move to the TV. I step back. I rush to the TV and crash the bat into the screen. The TV explodes and vomits all its shit on my living room floor.

I hammer the bat into the dining table near the oven. There's no dent. I hit it again. And again. I drive the bat into a leg and the table tilts over.

There's a full-length mirror in front of the door. I take aim. I heave back and hear the mirror crashing. Now the floor has a thousand mirrors.

There's a knock on the door. So I shut up and wait.

I am not breathing. There is another knock.

Krantik? Krantik? Open the door. Are you inside? It's Leonardo. I have the keys. I'm coming in.

So I slide open the door.

He walks in. He's not in uniform. Now I'm sitting on my couch and I've put the bat on the low-slung chairs I bought last month.

He walks gingerly over the destruction spilled all over the room. I'm sitting and not looking at him, because I don't particularly want to see anyone right now.

What happened?

I look to the left, away from him. The Bosch painting is in front of me. Men, women, and beasts run naked through the three panels in a hellish pursuit of pleasure. Everyone and everything is fucking each other. *The Garden of Earthly Delights*.

I'm not leaving, Krantik. What happened?

I'm sorry, I mutter. I damaged some stuff. The TV and the oven are mine. I'll pay you for the table and the mirror.

Forget the mirror. What happened to you?

Now he's removed the bat and is sitting in front of me. He's taller than me, so when he's on the low Ikea chair his face is level with mine.

Nothing.

You can tell me.

I have nothing to say to you. Everything, everyone, is a lie. How do I face anyone?

He sighs and studies the painting. He's tapping his knees. That's a really ugly painting, he says.

Yes, it is.

The next time I go to Brazil, I'll get you a poster of one of their hot chicas. You can cover that up. I'll find a great poster for you. Would that be nice?

Yes, that would be nice.

I have to go feed the turtles now. I was out till late because Nonna wanted a late-night walk, so I had to go out with her. But she doesn't like to see me in normal clothes. She loves telling everyone that I'm such a hotshot pilot. She'll tell the supermarket counter girls, she'll tell the grocery store man, she'll even tell the TV that Leonardo's a top pilot.

Is that why you keep your uniform on? I ask, but he doesn't confirm, just stands up hurriedly.

Anyway, I have to go. The turtles get really upset when dinner's late.

He waits at the door while his boots crunch mirrors on the ground.

I've done a lot of living. Some of it hasn't been very honourable. But I've learnt a few things.

Such as what? I ask, still facing away from him.

Life is a lot like the Kim Kardashian phenomenon. There's no reason for it. There's no point to it. But it's there.

I turn around.

So there is no lie, he continues, because there is no truth.

So what do we do?

You find something to love.

That doesn't solve anything if it's another lie.

No it doesn't. But it's the most beautiful lie in the world.

After Leonardo leaves, I stay on the couch for some time. I can see the Roman temple walls through the window. In some time, they slowly change colour as the dawn leaks into the night. I get up and leave. I need some air. There's no point sleeping now. I have my operation in four hours.

When I walk past the corner of my building and away from Leonardo and his turtles, I see the ZZ Top homeless man. He's picking up cigarette butts from the ground. I stop near him.

Scusa. Scusa mi.

He looks up.

Dove è . . .

I speak English, he says.

Do you know where the Colosseo is?

Yes, it's straight ahead of you.

Oh, yes, thank you.

I pull out a cigarette and offer it to him. I walk away and he calls out.

Do you know what they say about the Colosseo?

What do they say?

They say: As long as the Colosseo stands, Rome will stay. If the Colosseo crumbles, then Rome will fall. And if Rome falls, the whole world will fall.

He takes a satisfied drag of his cigarette.

And then I ask him: Are you busy?

Does it look like I'm busy?

Do you want to go for a walk?

Sure. Where are we going?

To find something to keep the Colosseo up, I said. What's your name?

Sisyphus.

Cool, I'm Krantik, I said. And walked downhill with him to the pile of rocks that was the Colosseo.